Bristol Short Story Prize:
The Winners

tangent
books

In Loving Memory of
Liz Corbett, Angela Sansom and John Sansom

Bristol Short Story Prize: The Winners

First published 2024 by Tangent Books

Tangent Books
Unit 5.16 Paintworks, Bath Road, Bristol BS4 3EH

www.tangentbooks.co.uk

Email: richard@tangentbooks.co.uk

ISBN: 9781914345340

Cover designed by Sarah Scyner
www.sarahscyner.com

Layout designed by Dave Oakley, Arnos Design
www.arnosdesign.co.uk

Printed in the UK by CMP, Poole on paper from a sustainable source

A CIP catalogue record for this book is available from the British Library
www.tangentbooks.co.uk

Introduction

What a joy it is to mark the beginning of an exciting new phase in the life of the Bristol Short Story Prize by publishing an anthology of the 16 stories that have won first prize in the competition's first 16 years.

Within these pages you will find a glorious mix of stories from writers in many different parts of the world. Assembling them together for the first time provides a great opportunity to approach the stories in a new light.

The short story is an ever-evolving and expanding form that defies definition. From the birth of BSSP we wanted to encourage writers to show us what is possible in a short story, what type of storytelling feats and wonder might be achieved without imposing any 'shoulds' or 'shouldn'ts', or 'how tos' or 'dos' and 'don'ts.'

And what a huge range of entries we have received over the 16 years the competition has been running. Stories set throughout history from ancient Greece to the present day, and beyond to imagined futures; stories narrated by centurions, by children not yet a decade old, and others with narrators and protagonists at all stages of life in between. Stories written in the first, second and third persons, with the broadest sweep of styles and genres: historical, romance, speculative, classic realism, dystopian, surreal flights of fancy, tense thrillers, comic capers, those that play with the form and idea of a 'story', those that might be said occupy the fiction/non-fiction hinterland, sparsely written hammer blows of just a few hundred words; stories set in countries all over the globe, penned by writers based in scores of different countries.

As well as receiving this very broad panorama of stories, one of the most pleasing aspects of running BSSP has been witnessing the number of writers who have gone on to further publication, been signed by agents, and reached many, many more readers after appearing in BSSP anthologies. The 16 winning stories gathered here include some of those writers. Their stories capture many of the subjects, themes, dilemmas and questions writers have probed and scrutinised in the entries we have received.

The brilliant anthology cover was designed by 3rd year Illustration degree student, Sarah Scyner, who is about to complete her course at the University of the West of England here in Bristol. The annual project we run with the students has been a very important part of our yearly activity; enormous thanks to course tutors, Chris Hill and Jonathan Ward, and all the students – we really hope this fruitful collaboration continues.

We are indebted to all the readers who have digested and deliberated over the thousands of entries we've received during these 16 years. A major thank you to all of them for their amazing commitment and graft, and for ensuring we have been able to publish and reward such memorable pieces of work.

Huge thanks, also, to all the judges who have studiously and respectfully approached the task of selecting shortlists and winning stories. The ferocious care and consideration which they all brought to the discussions produced 16 dazzling and dynamic anthologies.

Biggest thanks of all goes to everyone who has entered the competitions; what a thrill it has been to read and think about your creations. We can't express how much you have enriched and added to our lives.

As the competition moves to a new home under the guidance and stewardship of Dr Samantha Matthews and Dr Mimi Thebo of Bristol University's Department of English, this is a celebration of BSSP's first age and a toast to its future. We wish BSSP and its new guardians well. May it continue publishing and supporting brilliant writers long into the future. May it never stop fanfaring the wonderful form of the short story and providing scintillating reading experiences.

Lu Hersey, Richard Jones, Mike Manson, Bertel Martin, Catherine Mason, Joe Melia

*All profits from the sale of this anthology will be donated to the charities, Doctors Without Borders and Borderlands, a refugee charity based in Bristol.

Dima Alzayat

Dima Alzayat is the author of *Alligator and Other Stories* (Picador), a finalist for the PEN/Robert W. Bingham Prize for Debut Short Story Collection, the James Tait Black Memorial Prize, and the Swansea University Dylan Thomas Prize. Her short stories have appeared on BBC Radio 4, Esquire, Foyle's, Adroit, and Prairie Schooner. She holds a PhD in creative writing from Lancaster University, and was the 2022-23 Lillian Gollay Knafel Fellow at Harvard University's Radcliffe Institute for Advanced Study. Dima won the 2017 Bristol Short Story Prize.

GHUSL

U nder the bright lights the skin had turned a whitish gray. A bandage wrapped around the face kept the mouth closed and flattened the black hair, made the chin thick and shapeless and pushed the cheeks towards shut lids. Rolled towels beneath the head and neck lifted the shoulders slightly from the metal bed, and under the white sheet the big toes were strung together with twine.

I will do it myself, she had said. *Haraam, haraam,* the men had replied and she had laughed inches from their faces. *And what is this? Is this not also sin?* They had waited with her for the coroner's van, had unlocked the room and shown her where the materials were kept. After they lifted and placed him on the table the eldest among them turned to her once more. *Sister, let us prepare him.* The rest shifted their eyes as she moved closer to the table, uncovered his face and asked them to leave.

Towels and sheets, white and folded, were stacked on the counter next to a plastic bucket and washcloths. She washed her hands in the sink and let the hot water run until her fingers became red and raw, the rough soap granules burrowing beneath her nails. When she put the gloves on they were tight and pinched her damp skin and she pulled them off and set them on the counter. The hygiene mask stayed in its box and the incense stick stood unlit in its holder.

With a washcloth wrapped around her hand she lifted the half-filled bucket and turned towards the table where he lay. The skin to her looked coated in silver dust, like the ashes that remain after the burning of a great tree. *Up we go.* With her right hand at the nape of his neck she lifted his head and shoulders and with the left slowly and gently pressed down on his stomach, keeping cloth between fingers and skin. Several times she pressed and released, and without completely lifting the sheet wiped and cleaned between the legs in short, quick moves. *Hanna who is small*

> *fell*
>
> *in a well* *he got stung by wasps*
>
> *poor Hanna*
>
> *poor Hanna*
>
> *how*
>
> *did*
>
> *you*
>
> *fall?*

Again at the counter she washed her hands and cleaned the bucket. Even with her back to him she could still see his face. The thin closed lids and the green eyes beneath them, the muscle that strained against the skin and made it pliant to its shape. If she stood very still she could see him sit up on the steel table and swing his legs over its edge. He would look around and catch his image in the mirror on the wall. *How funny I look ya Zaynab.* She gripped the counter to steady herself as warm water filled the bucket.

Where are you?
When she turned around he was still on his back, the green eyes shut and the lips a pale violet. *Look at us playing hide and seek, even now.* She carried the bucket and a clean washcloth to the table and set them down, took her time wetting the cloth, dipping it into the bucket and squeezing it several times until there was nothing left to do but begin. She moved the sheet and looked at the hands once so small. *Give me your hand ya Hamoud.* Cleaning now between the fingers of hands bigger than hers, moving from the smallest to the thumb.

this is Mr. Tall
and useless

this is the
labneh licker

and this is
the ring wearer

This is uncle
Abu Hatem

this is the
nit killer.

She wet the washcloth again and touched it to the forehead and slowly worked it over the eyes, the moisture clinging to thick lashes, and down the nose, her hand hesitating above the faded scar that began at the bridge and zigzagged down to the right and disappeared. He was three when he had fallen and she was nine and she had been chasing him up and down the hallway when he slipped on the black and white tiles and his giggles turned to wails. She had picked him up and held him as blood gushed from the wound between his eyes. He had clung on to her so tightly, had pulled on the skin of her neck as he cried, would not release her even when their father came running into the room.

Her eyes moved to the top of the head, the gauze that covered, concealed. *We'll clean it*, the hospital nurse had said. She had wanted to say *No*, dizzied by the thought of more hands she did not know, touching and prodding and taking. Now, her eyes fixed on the cloth until she willed them to shift, to follow instead the washcloth she ran over each arm, right and then left, flattening the small hairs against the skin. Within seconds they began to dry and she watched them shrink back into curls. She looked at the hair on her own arms, not much lighter or finer, and a smile flashed across her face and disappeared. Neither one wanting to wait for the other, they used to stand side by side at the sink to make wudu before prayer, take turns running arms beneath the faucet, carrying with cupped hands water to wet their hair and clean their mouths and noses, their necks and ears.

She waited for her breath to steady before her hand again reached towards the bandage and this time worked around it, wiping the black hair that jutted out in thick locks. Hair that once was combed back and gelled, or let loose and framed the face, played against the skin. She held her hand still and inhaled, reached the cloth's corner below the bandage and cleaned behind one ear and then the next, circled their grooves and ridges. *Even now you tickle me ya Zaynab.* She could hear the low giggle that clambered in pitch and tumbled into a steady roll, the sounds coming closer together, the depth of the final laugh that allowed her to exhale. When she moved to the feet, she put the cloth down and with her wet hands washed one foot at a time, reached between the toes, and massaged each sole.

The men should do this, they had insisted while waiting for the van to arrive.

And who are they to me, these men? Or to him?

Still they persisted. *You will need more people, Ms. Zaynab. Three or four, at least, to lift and turn and wrap.*

I have lifted him before, she had hissed. *I will remember how to do it, Inshallah.*

The bucket again cleaned and re-filled, she dropped from her palm the ground lote leaves they had given her. She watched the green powder float on the water's surface. *Will you be dust now ya Hamoud?* She stood beside the table and looked at his face. When they were children he would sometimes lie still while they took turns playing surgeon and patient and whoever moved or laughed first when poked with plastic knives or tickled with cotton swabs would lose. *Let's wash you.*

Upper right side and then upper left, she knew, then bottom right and left. Head to toe. From his body the water trickled down into the table's grooved perimeter, ran down to the opening that drained into a second bucket placed there. She held her breath as she loosened the bandage and paused to watch the mouth. When she saw that the lips stayed closed, a sound left her own mouth, a sigh that escaped from the floor of her chest and burst the room's stillness. She would not lift the bandage completely, would not with her hands touch where she knew the bones would give, where tissues and nerves like sponges would sink beneath her fingers. From the cloth she squeezed enough water to wet what hair was visible, from her palm dribbled more over the back of the head. Down the neck and over the shoulder she worked the cloth, across the chest and down to the navel. When she tilted him on his left side so she could reach his back she was surprised at his weight, and felt her arm muscles strain to keep him from slipping.

The last time she had picked him up he was ten and reached her shoulders in height. Their father had not come home from work and her mother sat in the kitchen whispering into the telephone in between splintered sobs and breaths that dissolved in the cold air. She had found her brother on the living room carpet shaking. He had wet his pants and a silent panic had pinned him to the floor, would not let his body do anything but tremble like a final leaf on a winter tree. She hoisted him up, her arm around his waist, and asked him to walk. But his legs continued to quaver and she knew then he could not stand, and in one move lifted him and wrapped her arms around his legs. In the bathroom she undressed him and sat him in the bathtub, and only when she made the deep low sounds of a freight ship and splashed her hands like fish pirouetting out of the water did the shaking stop.

Keeping the sheet over his torso she reached beneath it, cloth wrapped around her fingers, and cleaned underneath and between the legs, down the right leg to the toes and then the left. Thoughts of unknown hands that might have touched where she now did, their intentions different and beyond the things she knew, she forced from her mind. A strangeness remained in their place. She knew she would have to repeat it all. Three times, five times, nine. *Until you smell like the seventh heaven, like Sidrat al-Muntaha itself.* But with each repetition, her hand grew less certain, what it felt unfamiliar, and she glanced several times at the face in reminder as she wiped.

When she filled the bucket one last time, the colorless camphor dissolved in the water and released a smell that reminded her of mothballs and eucalyptus, of rosemary and berries. She removed the sheet still covering him and left only the small cloth spread from navel to knees. In the fluorescent light his bared body looked long and broad, and she thought of once-smaller hands she had cupped in hers, narrower shoulders she had held. From head to feet she poured the water and inhaled the scent that rose as the water ran along the table's gutter and splashed inside the plastic bucket.

I saw a butterfly with my eyes

> *flitting*
> *it was   around*
> *me*

>   *I ran trying to catch it, but it   escaped*
> *from my hands.*

>   *Where is the butterfly?*
>   *It flew*

>   *away.*

She unfolded one of the large towels and began to dry him. Gently she lifted his head, dried his hair one thick lock at a time, felt the water soak through the cotton and onto her hands. The skin of her fingertips shriveled from so much water. *They might never dry again ya Hamoud.*

The day they returned her father, with clenched fists her mother had beaten her own chest, pulled handfuls of hair from her scalp until the neighbors came. Her brother screamed for doctors until a neighbor came running and pulled him away. She was old enough to know that no doctors were needed, that what now lay in the courtyard, covered in burns and cuts and skin that curled back to reveal shredded muscle and blood clotted and congealed was a body she no longer knew.

She stepped back and looked at the body before her now, clean and damp. She scanned for places she had missed, where she might again pour the water and run the cloth. At the sound of the door opening behind her she moved closer to the table before turning to see the same older man from before, the only one who had spoken to her. A younger man followed and between them they wheeled a table, smaller and without grooves. She stepped aside and stood silent as they positioned it next to the table where he lay, but when the younger one began to unfold the stacked shrouds, she drew closer, placed her hand on his and made it still. With eyes wide he pulled his hand away and stepped back, but when he opened his mouth to speak, the older man leaned towards him and whispered words that kept him quiet. *Wallah they don't know what to make of this ya Zaynab.* She could hear the amused tone, the smile in the voice.

Two large sheets she unwrapped and placed, one atop the other, on the empty table. The smaller sheet she carried to where he lay, and unfolded over his body as they watched. Her hands hesitated when the sheet reached his neck and she could not lift all of him at once, she knew. She drew back enough to allow the men to move to either side of her, her fists clenching at her sides when with gloved hands they reached for him. As they lifted him the neck gave way and the head tilted back and she pressed her feet to the concrete floor. After they lowered him onto the second table and the head again rested flat, the older man reached beneath the sheet and removed the cloth covering the thighs. The younger man gripped the sheet's corners and began to pull it higher. She moved towards him. Stood close enough to feel the youthful swell of his belly protrude and recede with each breath, to make out the nose hairs that shivered as he drew air. Again the older man intervened, held the younger by the elbow and led him towards the door.

With the soil still new on her father's grave, they had come for her brother. Men with masked faces and heavy boots who slapped her grandfather across the face and threatened to tear off her clothes as her mother watched. *And like a good boy you sat so quietly.* In the kitchen cupboard behind pots and jars and sacks of rice and flour. When they left they took her grandfather with them, and the blood drops from her mother's nose spread like petals on the tiles.

She stood now at the counter mixing the sandalwood paste in a small bowl. Over and over she inhaled the scent and tried to keep her hands steady. *You will smell like the earth, ya Hamoud, like a tree and its soil.* Back where he lay, his face still uncovered, with her fingers she dabbed the paste onto his forehead and nose and rubbed it in, but still the brown tinted his pale face. With his hand in hers she worked the paste into one palm and then the next, reached beneath the sheet and dabbed the knees, and then the feet. She wished it were her feet on the table, her legs, her body. Imagined his hands stained brown as he touched her forehead instead. But his face, as she imagined it, contorted in silent grief, pushed the thought from her mind.

The three of them had arrived in a new country seeking darkness, the quiet of unlit rooms and the absence of knocks. A place where names had no meaning. Together they searched for the missing pieces of their mother, the stories that had shed their words. Not knowing why, she felt relief when he grew taller and bigger than she was. When he was found in the early morning hours behind the shop where he worked,

his skull opened and spilling blood that ran through the black hair and onto the asphalt, she had been the one to call for doctors.
I had a little bird.

I looked after him,

and when his feathers grew and he was big,
he started to peck my cheeks

Zik   zik   zik   zik
zeek

Gently now she bent the left arm so that the palm flattened against the chest, folded the right arm so that the right palm rested on the left. *And this is how we pray ya Hamoud.* When he was six she had taught him how to pray. Her parents laughed that he was too young, but she had spent years waiting for him to grow, to learn words and what they meant, so that she could show him things, teach him what she knew; the alphabet and how to ride a bike, the names of animals alive and extinct, the planets in the solar system and their moons. So when she stood beside him on the prayer rug and told him to move as she did, he did as he was told, touching hands to chest and then to knees, forehead touching the carpet and back up again. For years after he would only pray if she led.

She stood beneath the bright lights, her fingertips grazing the sheet's edge. Her eyes traced the arc of his brows, the hairs that strayed from their place. She imagined what they looked like when he smiled, the way they drew together, and noticed for the first time the thin lines near his eyes. *Whose eyes will see us now?* Her mother, she knew, would never speak again. Her own words as she pulled the sheet above the mouth and then higher still were like boats with neither sails nor oars.

After the sheets were wrapped around him, the center looped with ropes, the ends fastened, she stood with empty hands. *Make me like a sandwich ya Zaynab.* She would have him lie on the bed sheet and roll him from one end to the other, and through the layers she could hear his giggles. If her mother or father were walking by, they laughed with them. *Make sure he can breathe ya Zaynab.*

John Arnold

Johnny Arnold was raised in Far North Queensland, Australia. He began writing as an escape after being interred in a Brisbane boys' Catholic school. After university, he lived and wrote variously in Melbourne, Europe and Bristol – however he only found his voice as an author after writing about his hometown. The resulting story, *Naked as Eve*, won the Bristol Short Story Prize in 2012. His short fiction *Skeleton Creek* has since been included in the 2021 Faber Anthology. He is the author of five plays that have been produced by Melbourne theatre company, Move Create Dance. His 2022 play, *Blood Makes Noise* was the subject of the documentary The Kids Play by director Libby Chow. His most recent plays, *Perfect Day* and *The Singularity* are being produced in April this year. He's currently finishing a full-length mystery novel set in the Far North. He's a husband, a father of two and the owner of a dingo named Boudicca. Instagram @johnnylarnold.

NAKED AS EVE

No-one around here really believes in curses. It's just tourism. It sells fridge magnets and tea towels. Books out more tours than the bunyip or the min-min lights. Howie tells me 'curse' isn't the right word anyway and neither is 'spell.'

He says: 'It's a white colonial attempt to trivialise Aboriginal spirituality exacerbated by the rank stupidity of tourists. Darling, the tourists! I had a German ask me if he could feed a cassowary. A fucking cassowary. They think it's Eurodisney with scuba diving. Don't bogart that ganga.'

Twice weekly his mini-bus rattles through the town: prompting laughter and flicked cigarettes from the wrecks marinating under the pub's ceiling fans; cueing Naomi at the corner shop to dust off a cardboard box full of boomerangs and diligently peel off their 'made in Taiwan' stickers. The bus squeaks to a halt near the creek and disgorges tourists into the stupefying heat.

Howie always chooses his ensemble carefully: khaki shorts and shirt, an akubra, brown legs encased in socks and sturdy boots. He waves away imaginary flies and leads them to the pool, filling the silence with the accented chatter they expect.

'Yep, me Mum's people bilonga mountains round here (careful of the batshit there, Missus) me Grandad was the last blackfella hung for spearing a white. Over at Murdering Point. Nah, it's named after a shipwreck: survivors ate each other. Bloody good tucker. Whitefella from the museum found a ribcage with human teeth-marks last month. Wouldn't lean on that tree – ants bigger than your head. Lotta archaeological interest in this area. Did I tell ya 'bout Palmer Kate's solid-gold chamber pot? Here we go.'

The pool is framed by robber ferns and logs furred with moss. The roots of massive trees seem to cup the water in lichen spotted hands. Woody vines are spun like lace from tree to tree. On a hot day, the water seems as clear and tempting as vodka with ice.

The tourists groan with relief. The cool of the forest is like a kiss against the skin, a kind of blessing. With sweat cooling in their waistbands, with their skin no longer blossoming red, the other backpackers don't seem as annoying, their hostels don't seem as nasty, the accents don't seem as jarring.

One or two scamper down to the edge, dip their fingers and splash water on their faces.

'Bloody nice, eh?' Howie grins. 'Not a bad backyard.'

There's a titter of laughter. Scandinavians, sunburned to the colour of coffee, think about swimming. Americans, merely sunburned, wait to be impressed.

Howie falls silent. He lets them slowly feel the cold, lets them slowly notice the quiet.

He clears his throat. 'The first whitefella to disappear here (that's the first we know about) was in 1898. He'd just proposed to his girlfriend. Daughter of a local landowner. They were sittin' exactly where we are now. Dressed all in white. Big hats and a silver teapot. Blackfella servants lookin' out for snakes and serving scones.'

An English girl looks at her shoes. She smiles apologetically.

'The blackfellas, they been nervy all afternoon. One of 'em won't leave the carriage. One of 'em, the cups rattle every time she pours the tea. The horse what bilonga whitefellas rears up and bolts. Girlfriend and the blackfellas run out to the road, but horsie's long gone. Where's the boyfriend?'

'They come back and Brother's in the water, swimming away from the shore with all his clothes on. The Missus she laughs. Thinks maybe he's joking. She calls for him. He can't hear her. Keeps swimming. She calls again. And again. He's downstream now, stumbling over rocks. Just down there where the water turns white.'

Howie indicates a bend in the creek, almost invisible in the forest gloom, where the current begins to hasten.

'Blackfellas they know about sacred places. Know about spirits. Know it's time to leave. They try and take Missus with them. Crying, pulling at her hand, pulling at her skirt. She won't go. Not leaving without Brother.'

'Ranger finds her the next day. Dress ripped and muddy. Face and hands all scratched. Sunburned and crazy. She won't say what happened. Just mutters to herself. Screams when they try and take her from the water.'

Someone asks what happened to the fiancé.

Howie smiles.

'Never found Brother. No body. Nothing.'

Someone else suggests crocodiles.

'No crocs in this creek. Too bloody cold.'

Howie pauses. The tourists notice the silence, the stillness of the water, the absence of fish.

'Missus died a few years later in a hospital in Brisbane. Wouldn't eat or wash herself. Family had her put away. She never said nothing. Just used to mutter the same thing over and over, like a scratched CD.'

An American clears his throat. 'What did she say?'

'She says "Naked as Eve." Howie stops and looks at his audience. 'Everyday for years all she says is "Naked as Eve."'

There's another silence.

Howie waits for the inevitable question: 'What does that mean?'

He pulls a sheet of paper from his bag.

'Before they locked her away, Missus used to paint. Wouldn't speak, but she'd sit on her veranda with her paintbrushes, muttering to herself. They had one of her watercolours at a Uni down in Brisbane. This is a copy.'

It could be a coloured plate from an old copy of Tennyson. A graceful forearm with a delicate wrist is rising from still water. She could be the lady of the lake but there's no Excalibur and our fairy is brown-skinned. Closer scrutiny reveals the pink colouring of her palm and the pandanus leaf behind her. In the foreground, a man's straw hat floats on the surface of the water.

The backpackers look at each other. Some giggle and some glance around the clearing.

As the coup de grace, Howie brings out the photos.

'This,' he says, 'is a photo of Brother. His name was Charles Anderson.'

A black and white photo is passed around the group. It's a posed, studio portrait of a man with a hawk nose and swept-back, blonde hair.

'And this,' says Howie, 'is a photo of Missus. Her name was Nora Palmer.'

Another photo circulates: a kind of mug shot. A woman with black, matted hair is turning away from the camera. She's painfully thin and there's a rip in the shoulder of her dress. Her bottom lip is slack, her expression infantile. She is unmistakably mad.

'These are the first two victims of the Witch's Pool.'

Howie smiles, 'Any of you whitefellas wanna swim?'

The tourists laugh.

Of course, it's all bullshit.

Howie is dabbing clear polish onto his nails. The smell of acetone mingles unpleasantly with the reek of pot.

'Things a bitch has to do to make a living. Honestly darling, maybe I should get a job on the Skyrail?'

I take another long drag and say, 'You don't know anything about marsupials and ferns and shit.'

He motions for the joint, takes a drag and blows a smoke ring.

'I know platypuses' anuses are also their vaginas. They're called cloacas. I think that's where we get the word clacker.'

We both start to giggle.

'Clacker, darling,' he says. 'Clacker, clacker, clacker.'

We're at my dining table, drinking beer. Sweat runs from my hairline, down my back and into my jeans. Strings of bud and bush tobacco are dusted over the table's surface. I notice the black mould has started creeping over the louvres again. Through the cracks, white sunshine stabs at the dimness of the house.

Howie says, 'Sorry about your Dad, eh?'

I reclaim the joint. 'I've been trying to feel sorry. Mainly, I'm just relieved.'

I know there's something missing in me. A good person wouldn't feel this way.

Howie says, 'Let's hope he's nicer to the new wife.'

I laugh. 'Hope, they say, springs eternal.'

'Oh honey,' Howie drips polish onto a knuckle. 'They say all kinds of shit.'

Mum is walking down the hall towards us. The first thing I notice is the dirt on her feet. I want to mop the floor till it shines.

'G'day Marie,' Howie says. 'You look deadly.'

Mum is wearing her nightie and a winter coat. Her face is wet and sweat has left patches on her stomach. She's wearing bright red lipstick.

'Olivia,' she says. 'You should ask your little half-caste friend if his Mummy would like any of my old clothes.'

Howie glances at me. His smile drops.

'Mum,' I say. 'This is Howie. You remember Howie? From school?'

She holds out her hand like the Queen at the opening of a hospital. 'How do you do.'

Howie shakes her hand. 'How do you do, Mrs. Rossi.'

Mum says, 'I let Tony Tedeleschi put his hand in my undies.'

Howie chokes and starts coughing.

'Sorry,' he says. 'Fuck, sorry.'

I rub my eyes. 'Mum, are you tired? Do you want a sleep?'

She shakes her head 'It hurt and he said he wouldn't tell anyone. Sorry! I'm sorry!'

I take a long breath. 'It's okay Mum. It's okay.'

I stand up and put my hand on her arm. She looks at me like a curious bird, makes a little twittering sound. She swings and I don't have time to duck. Her hand connects with my jaw, makes my teeth snap together.

'You know where your father is! You've seen them together! You tell me! Tell me! He has to come back!'

I put my hands over my head. She's weak but she sometimes goes for the eyes. Howie is on his feet and has his arms around her. He's pulling her away.

'It's cool, Mrs. Rossi! Let's all chill the fuck out! It's cool!'

My hair is caught in her fingers and I'm saying, 'Mum! Mum! Mum, Mum, Mum…'

'Let's be cool!'

'Tell me!'

I notice the joint is smouldering unattended on the floor-boards.

'He's with that little black gin!' Mum's kicking now. Howie has his arm around her waist. 'He can't! He has to come back! Filthy little lubra!'

'Is it just me,' Howie says, 'or have you gotten more racist lately?'

I can't help it: I start to laugh. Then Howie starts and soon we're bent over and gasping, wiping away tears. Mum is wrong-footed. She stops yelling. Glances around. She looks at me and the corner of her mouth tilts. She blinks.

'It's very hot.' She says.

'Yes,' I take a breath and straighten up. 'Would you like to take your coat off?'

She nods. I stand behind her, slip it from her shoulders. She's wet herself and I want to keep this from Howie. Mum wouldn't want a man to notice. I hold the coat over her sodden nightie.

'How about a shower, Mum? Cool you down?'

She nods, 'It's very hot.'

I gently lead her towards the bathroom.

Behind me, I hear Howie say, 'Fuck!'

But he's looking at his ruined nails.

Howie has designed a tea towel that's a masterpiece of the macabre.

The pool is depicted in its centre and is trimmed with the names of its alleged victims: Johann Becker 1974, James Whitelaw 1975, Dieter Webb 1976 and so on. In the bottom-right are the year 2011 and a question mark.

'Someone goes missing every year?' A girl with blonde hair and American accented English is buying souvenirs under Howie's tutelage.

'Not every year, Missus.' Howie says, tilting back his akubra. 'Hotaka Sato he went in '95 and then Brad Johnson well he didn't bloody go till what? '98?'

'He went in '97,' Naomi corrects him from the counter. 'Nice bloke. Sold him a didgeridoo and a packet of condoms.'

Howie ignores her.

'Y'see sista, back in the dreaming my people knew they had to keep the Witch happy. Some poor old bugger offered himself up every now and then. And if no-one offered, someone got the short-straw, got biffed over the head and thrown in. But they didn't have years. Didn't have time like you whitefellas. But they knew the pool demanded its sacrifices.'

The girl touches his arm. 'You're like, really spiritual.'

At the counter, Naomi mimes vomiting.

I hand over my purchases: tampons, milk, tea.

'Human sacrifice is new,' she whispers.

'But not unwelcome,' I whisper back, 'depending on the human.'

The cash register sings and the change draw kicks out.

'Heard your Dad pissed off to Cairns with some scrag. Sucks arse, eh?'

I nod. Look at the counter for a little too long. Force myself to speak.

'It was Bowen. He went to Bowen.'

'True?

I glance up at her. Naomi flicks open a plastic bag.

'It's a relief honestly. He was so horrible to Mum.'

'True?'

'He wanted to sell the house and put Mum in a home.'

'Oh true? What an arsehole. Y'know,' Naomi leans forward, taps the counter with her acrylic nails. 'I always thought your Dad was a dodgy prick. Didn't like the way he looked at me when I slept over your place. Better off without him, darl.'

She smiles at me and says, 'You're a good daughter, Liv.'

I look up at her face. She hasn't really changed in twenty years. She still has all the certainties of childhood. Still doesn't realise what people are capable of.

I say, 'Mum would never have survived in a home.'

Naomi hands me my change.

'So, who is she?'

My car keys jingle on the counter.

'Who?'

There's a moment's pause and she tilts her head.

'Your Dad's skank. Who is she?'

I'm momentarily without words. I smile and open my mouth. Nothing comes out.

'You can tell me, darl,' Naomi says. She makes a show of locking her lips with an imaginary key. 'Tracey at my hairdressers reckons it's one of those southern sluts who come up here for Easter and can't keep their legs together. But I reckon whoever she is, she's a local.'

I play with my keys and clear my throat.

'Yeah. Yeah, she's a local.'

'True?' Naomi covers her mouth. 'I fucking knew it. Who is it? Not Bree from the Green Frog?'

I shake my head and pick up my bag.

Naomi says, 'Well of course it's not Bree. She has like the worst tropical ulcers. Who is it?'

I repeat her earlier gesture: mime locking my lips and dropping the key into my cleavage.

She laughs, 'I'll get it out of ya darl: a cone, a couple of wines and you'll break like a hymen on a Contiki tour.'

I think about Mum. Think about what she said that night.

I say, 'As silent as the grave, love. I'll be as silent as the grave.'

Mum has burned her hand taking a cake out of the oven without mitts. She's marvelling over her palm's seared, shiny surface when the phone rings.

'Hello?'

'Is Bruno Rossi there, please?' It's a male voice: broad with hard vowels.

Sweat trickles down the side of my face. I take a breath.

'Olivia!' Mum calls. 'Turn off Press Gang and do your homework!'

'Hello? This is Constable Reilly from the Innisfail Police.'

A drop of sweat stains the floorboards. I can hear Mum rummaging in the kitchen drawers.

'Hello,' I clear my throat. 'Sorry. Um, Bruno Rossi isn't at this address anymore.'

I can hear him sigh – it's Friday and he's impatient to be at the pub, sinking schooners and chatting up backpackers.

'This is the last address registered for a white, 2004 Toyota Hilux registered to Bruno Rossi. Correct?'

'Yes,' I say. 'But he doesn't live here anymore. Or visit. With or without his car.'

There's a moment of silence.

'And I suppose,' Constable Reilly yawns, 'you don't have his current address?'

Glass shatters in the kitchen.

'Ooopsy daisy,' says my mother.

'I don't, Constable,' I say. 'Men who abandon their families are often behind on those little details. What's this about, please?'

There's a pause.

'Look, I'm really just calling to inform someone that the car's being impounded for illegal parking and about a month's worth of unpaid parking fines. If he wants it back, he better get in contact.'

The phone's wet against my ear. I shift it to the other side.

'So you've found Dad's car.'

'Yeah,' the Constable sighs. 'Now we're cookin' with gas. Still no idea where he is?'

I long to tell the worthy Constable to perform a sexual act upon his own person.

Instead I say, 'Cooktown. My father moved to Cooktown.'

Then I hang up.

It's cooler by the time I put Mum to bed, but her nightie is already damp against her skin. In case she needs me in the night, I make sure the mosquito net is loose around the mattress.

She pulls something from under her pillow. It looks about the size of a notebook.

'Tell your father I found his wallet.'

The net slips from my hands. I straighten up.

'What was that, Mum?'

'His wallet,' Mum says. 'I found it under the sink. He says I'm stupid.

But he's daft really.'

I put my head inside the netting.

'I'll give it to him if you like. When he's home from work.'

She passes me a leather wallet. It's soft, brown and well-used. I flip it open. His licence and all his cards are still inside. I let out a breath, drop my shoulders.

Mum rolls onto her side.

'You're not stupid, Mum.' I kiss her on the cheek. She smells like rose soap.

I turn off the light. Mum sits upright, grabs for me through the net.

'You were there,' she says.

For a moment, I listen to the geckoes kiss at each other across the ceiling.

'What?' It's important not to encourage her. 'Go to sleep, Mum.'

'You were there at the pool.'

The pulse starts in my neck. I breathe out slowly.

'Mum, you've been dreaming. You were asleep.'

'You planned it together,' she says. 'You and that gin. You let her have him.'

I've told myself a hundred times that there's no need to panic. But my face feels cold and I want to vomit.

'I don't know what you're talking about, Mum. You've been dreaming.'

Of all the things she could remember. Not my birthday, not the year, not that flesh is vulnerable to flame. No: she remembers that night.

Mum is staring at me.

'He was going to leave, Mum,' I say. 'He was going to put you in a home.'

The geckoes are growing louder, but I think I hear Mum laugh.

She settles back onto her pillows.

'Naked as Eve,' she says. 'She was naked as Eve.'

No-one around here really believes in curses. We're a practical people. We know that old creek can run cold enough to cramp muscles, make a swimmer's limbs turn white and useless. We know the creek can take dogs and horses. Some of us have seen wallabies caught by the current, seen them thrash, turn cold and sluggish, and then go under. We know the creek can summon a frozen current from underground and swallow a corpse whole. Some of us have watched a body spin in the pool, watched the current play with it, watched as it disappeared into the creek's roaring, white mouth. Mum would have never survived in a home. And like Howie says, the pool demands its sacrifices.

Emily Bullock

Emily Bullock won the Bristol Short Story Prize in 2011 with her story *My Girl*, which was also broadcast on BBC Radio 4. Her short stories have been featured in different anthologies including *A Short Affair* (Scribner, 2018). She has an MA in Creative Writing from the University of East Anglia and completed her PhD at the Open University, where she is a senior lecturer in Creative Writing. Her debut novel, *The Longest Fight*, was shortlisted for the Cross Sports Book Awards, and listed in *The Independent's* Paperbacks of the Year 2015. Her second novel, *Inside the Beautiful Inside* was published in 2020, and her collection of short stories, *Human Terrain*, was published in 2021 and longlisted for the Edge Hill Prize 2022. Her novella, *For Always Only*, will be published by Reflex Press in 2024.

MY GIRL

My job is to stop the blood, cool her off, wash her down. Who knows her better than her own mum? I rub the yellow car wash sponge across her head, smooth my fingers over the braids, sweeping away water with the back of my hand. Her coach leans over the ropes, whispering words I can't hear. All I have to do is make sure the match isn't stopped for bleeding. I open a jar and rub adrenalin chloride into the cut on her right cheek. Old scar tissue has ripped open, isn't much blood, but I'm not taking chances. My girl keeps her eyes on the other corner, but she lets me move her face from side to side, checking for fractures. Clean. An eyelash drops and curls onto my finger. I make a wish and send it on its way. The bucket of icy water has clouded pink but her reflection is steady. Nobody hears my wish.

Time is nearly up. I collect the bucket, towel and my toolbox of potions. I sit back down on the other side of the ring where it is darker, small pools of pale light collecting under the lamps on each table. I am one of them again: spectator. My girl stretches her arms and legs, letting the ropes take her weight, in the last seconds of rest. But the ring isn't empty. The men cheer as the bikini bulging girl, slipping in her white slingbacks, parades with the first round card held high above her yellow perm; howls loud as dogs left chained in a backyard, the air cold with moans.

I rub blue sanitizer into my hands. I don't want any dirt to get onto her broken skin. The liquid evaporates quick as tears; it smells as tart as the gin and tonics splashed across the tablecloths behind me. This is an exhibition fight, but the money is good and it will keep her in gloves and membership for six months. My girl watches it all. She shakes her head and water hits the floor in front of my shoes. The man behind me orders another round of whiskies and a cheer goes up.

The bell for the second round deadens the noise for a moment. My girl comes out tight, keeping hits away from the red lump swelling above her kidney. Her opponent is a swarmer. She comes at my girl again, happy to take hits on the ride in. Whisky splashes against my neck as a man behind waves his glass in the air. But my girl is fast. She blocks the blows without turning; eyes watching her opponent's muscles. Ready to knock and duck. Bang. My girl lands a punch to the side of the head. She circles and steps off again. Reach for it, reach for it, a man screams from behind his stack of pints; myopic eyes blinking through the glass.

No backdoor nightclub scratching and slapping here. Some cheer and some snigger behind napkins as they dab steak juice from their lips. Swift footwork smears blood into the canvas, pinned shadows which the fighters move around. A left upper cut to her opponent's chin silences the crowd. Splatters of red spin over the ropes and smack the front row; a spot balloons on my jeans. The other fighter's knees lock, a real pro and she stays standing. She pulls back, elbow in for power and slugs my girl deep in the gut. I can't breathe for her, can't feed her from my body anymore. Her eyes narrow and she circles; playing for time as she sucks down air to free the hot cramping pain. Her blue singlet and shorts turn black with sweat. After the fight, tonight, I will tell her. Enough. My girl took the punches even when she was a swollen bulge inside me.

It was a blow to the stomach finally woke me up. I was expecting it, my hands wrapped around her hidden body, leaving my head uncovered. He raised his foot above my face, but something stopped him: the banging from the neighbours upstairs, a siren on the street. He slammed the hallway door so hard it bounced right open again, did the same with the front door. I held on to the broken back of the chair, sat up and felt my girl kick. I laughed: all those doors wide open.

A draught from the fire exit blows litter in off the street, a crisp packet and burger wrapper circle and settle by the bucket. I boot them away. The cold air is no good for her muscles, but no one will hear me if I shout at them to close it again. The green light glows through the grey soup of smoke and beer belches. I shake the clean towels, plumping air into the folds.

They are locked together, tugging apart at the referee's shout. Her heart is fair beating out of her chest. She snorts air, nostrils flaring. But she isn't slowing. Her lip doesn't droop, her eyes aren't blinking. It is a good sign. Her coach signals with his hands, their secret language: a combination of hits or a change of tactics. She won't tell me their code. And that makes me proud. I'm here because she wants me. She's long past needing me to pull up her socks, wipe her nose, trim her crusts. So I wait for the bell to go, fold my bandages, mix my ointments to stop the cuts flowing. Hands working automatically as I watch her spin and circle around the ring. Her stretched plaits reveal the soft pink of her scalp; fontanelle toughened over the years, but I remember the first warm pulsing.

On the 18th December 1989, when waves smashed Blackpool

pier and leaves whipped against windows, she began to fight. In the upstairs bathroom, on a blue fish and smiling dolphin beach towel, the ambulance delayed under a falling oak, my girl was born. She came out screaming: fists balled, face red, breathing hard. No one but me to hear her.

The bell goes for the third round. I am back at her side again. I squirt water into her mouth; collect it in the bucket as she spits it up. Wipe down her face and grease her skin to make the leather slide off. My nipples throb under the layers of jersey just like they did when she was a baby. I press a frozen eye iron to the top of her cheek, milking out the swelling. She lets me cradle her head, but tilts her ear towards the bell to better trap its sound.

She catches a couple of good hits in the third. One to the ribs. One to the back. A small cut is opening up under her right eye. It will need seeing to. She is hooking with her left and some of the men lean forward shouting encouragement, congratulating her coach. She's a born fighter, he tells them and waves his hand to show it is all he has to say.

I stood outside the gates on her first day of school, parents waving all around. And she asked me, what happened to my daddy? He was a fighter, I told her. If there were ever words I wish I could swallow back, they are it. The bruises he left me had long since yellowed and leaked away. She didn't ask anything else and I knew she'd get smart enough to fill in the rest. I watched her swing her orange PE bag over her shoulder and I waved until I thought my hands would drop off.

The fluorescent strip light coats her with its orange glue. With a right upper cut her opponent stuns her. I see her eyes as they flicker white. She glances over. All I can do is sit back and let it happen. The other fighter presses closer, forcing my girl's curling spine up against the ropes. Bang. Bang. Bang. A burst of hooks so fast, I'm not sure if I count three or four. But my girl won't go down. The light swings above the canvas, dividing up the ring, as they circle each other. Matched pound for pound, my girl stands an inch shorter than her opponent; but she meets her in the eye like they are the same height. No one has ever come close to knocking her down. Not that it stops me biting my lip and holding my breath.

When she was seventeen, out of school and out of work, she found her way to the gym. The boys there said, 'er's a funny 'un'. She didn't listen to them and went back every day it was open. She asked Bristol Pete, shoplifter to order, to fetch up some Everlast leather gloves, ten ouncers. I used to worry that she never came home until the sky outside the kitchen was one dark bruise, that welts and scrapes on her skin glowed red in the cold night air. I only let myself exhale when I heard her key in the lock. On Sundays she ran along the cold sucking sand, jumping dog shit the tide wasn't quick enough to wash away.

She swells in and out of the other fighter's reach, keeping in close and holding her guard up. My girl feints with a left and follows through with a smack from the right. She doesn't stay still to soak up the praise from the crowd. Feet seeming to float above the canvas as she pushes towards a neutral corner. My girl is punching smooth and fast, legs wide enough for balance but close enough that the petroleum jelly at the top of her thighs has rubbed off. Her skin will be turning red under those long silk shorts. My girl gets up close, ready to finish it. But her opponent isn't down yet; feet shuffling, shoulders dipping as she comes back at my girl. A deep blow under the belt, but they are too close, their bodies block the referee's view. Only I see it. That burning pain in her groin is spreading through her legs, slowing her down. She can't lower her hands, can't press the spot to deaden the pain. I crack an ice pack and get the water bucket ready. One sneaky left hook and bang, it could all be over for my girl too. Some punches in life you can't slip.

They're calling her The Blackpool Illuminator because she lights up the ring; that's what she told me over egg and chips, runny not set, a week before her first match. I knew why. It wasn't in her face, square and blunt like mine, or her hardened body. It was in the way she moved. Fork to mouth, knife to plate: stabbing out combinations, left and right. She pushed off from the balls of her feet as she got up to help me with the dirty plates. My girl balanced like a spinning top. I held my wrists under the cold water until I managed to squeeze out a smile for her.

The ice pack in my hand is numbing my skin. But I suck down hot air, whistling through my front teeth, as my girl takes a jab to the side of the face. Her head snaps back on her neck as the end bell goes. For one moment I taste the frozen silence of the hall, it fizzes and crackles on the heat of my tongue. But it isn't a sugared ice lolly taste. The points are totted up. The white shirted referee lifts an arm. Of course, the hometown fighter wins. Her fist smacks up into the air. The cheers aren't for my girl. Not this time. She slaps gloves with her opponent and crosses the canvas, back to me. But I keep my arms stiff at my side, so they can't open wide and pull her close.

Sweat runs into her eyes and she tries to flick at it with her gloves. I hold back her head and wipe her face dry with a fresh towel; press the ice pack to the base of her neck. I dab at the small cut under her eye, red and yellow, congealing already. Maybe if I hadn't wiped over her beginnings with that word, fighter, if she wasn't born in the great storm of '89, she wouldn't be up there now. But I can't imagine her any other way. Her opponent is carried off in a whirl of white teeth smiles and pumping arms. The audience is leaving, scraping chairs and slapping backs. I rub her down with the towels, cloak her body and legs. The men tug on jackets, sleeves turned inside out, fingers numbed by booze and legs deadened from steak and chips. 'I'll bring the car round,' her coach says as he gives her shoulder a pat.

A lone flash bulb bleaches her face. It's all done for the night. 'I lost,' she says. 'You didn't win this one but there'll be others,' I tell her. There won't be any story about my girl in The Echo, not tomorrow anyway. Search for her online and boxer puppies for sale from Blackpool kennels pops up. I hold open the ropes and she climbs out of the ring. She breathes in the coppery smack of blood, the taste of success. Together we walk through the blue ticket-stub and crumpled-napkin dust that the dinner jacket men have left behind. Sometimes we aren't the hero in our own stories: she fights and I stand in her corner, it's the way it will always be. Fists balled, face red. Breathing hard.

Isidora Cortes-Monroy

Born in Chile and raised in Switzerland, Isidora Cortes-Monroy has always navigated her intercultural world through literature. Her story, *His Back*, was selected as a runner up for the Jane Austen Literacy Foundation short story competition and was published as an Audible. In addition, her story, *The Scientific Method* was also selected for a short story anthology published by Leno and Bandini. Currently, she is completing her PhD at the University of Toronto, Canada.

CAKE FOR THE DISAPPEARED

I t didn't surprise me the first night Joaquin didn't come back. He was always one to come home late. On most occasions he would return early the next morning, but there had been instances when we wouldn't see him for days. My mother, on the other hand, knew from the start that this time was different. We told her she was being dramatic, that she needn't worry, Joaquin was like that. She remained unconvinced.

At ten o'clock on that first morning, my mother baked a cake. This one was Joaquin's favourite, a milhojas de manjar. My mother had a special way of making it: the trick was to toast several handfuls of walnuts, crush them and spread them evenly between every layer, giving the cake an unexpected crunch. Once she had put on the final layer and had sprinkled a generous serving of crushed walnuts on top, she placed it on our dining table, washed her equipment and prepared her ingredients for the next recipe. She then baked a batch of chilenitos. Once those were done, she made a pot of arroz con leche. As soon as she finished it, she moved onto her well known brazo de reina. She spent her day walking back and forth between the kitchen and the dining table, placing on its surface each new pastry. By the time night had fallen and dinner time approached, the table seemed to have disappeared, submerged under a sea of desserts. My father and I, too scared to get in the way of my mother's cooking, decided it would be too complicated to cook a real meal, so we settled for a batch of cuchuflis for dinner. We ate by the window, watching the streets for any sign of Joaquin.

Breakfast the next day was no different, save for the assortment of desserts available to us. My mother had spent the whole night baking. With no more room left for desserts on the dining table, my mother had begun leaving them on the floor. The tide of food had now started creeping into the living room. By midday, the sofas were taken up by numerous trays and plates carefully balanced on their cushions. They look like they're in a meeting, my Dad joked. I laughed and suggested we eat the group leader for lunch. For the second time in twenty-four hours we filled up on dessert, this time cutting into a postre de tres leches that bled condensed milk.

By the second day, my father began to worry this was more than just a phase. We were quickly running out of habitable space as well as growing tired of these sweet meals. The first thing he did that morning was buy me a proper breakfast from the local market, making sure that my food was packed with the protein and vitamins I hadn't been able to eat the day before. He then began taking the trays of pastries to different neighbors' houses, begging them to accept as many as five or six desserts at a time. By lunchtime he had visited all our neighbors, yet the pile of deserts continued to grow, creeping into every crevice and hiding spot the house had to offer. Nothing was beyond their reach. Exasperated with the situation, my father loaded his car with as many delicacies as he could fit and drove to the market, in the hopes that he could sell them away. I stayed at home monitoring the street outside our house, in case Joaquin should return. By the time my father came back, the guest room and his own bedroom had been refilled with a new series of cakes.

A week had passed and nothing had changed, save for the number of rooms occupied by pastries. I was no longer surprised when I found an alfajor on my desk or a bag of hallullas stuffed inside my sock drawer. My room was no longer my own. Despite my father's efforts to sell the produce at the market, the tide continued to grow, spreading itself out across the house. He began to realize that as long as his wife continued to bake, we would never be rid of all the desserts, not even with the help of our family and neighbors.

He decided then to open a shop in the center of Santiago and sell her cakes there. It had never been my parents' ambition to open up their own shop, nor had my mother ever shown a particular interest in selling her pastries. But my father was out of options, and so he bought the first property he could find. He named my mother's bakery after her, Dulce Soledad. It took him a day to put up a few shelves and find a cash register. Besides those few basic elements, my father believed nothing else would be needed to sell my mother's desserts. His biggest concern wasn't the decorations or the marketing, but rather how to get my mother out of the house and into the shop. Throughout the course of three days we moved her utensils, making sure to only move a few at a time. On the last day we left a bowl and a whisk as the last pieces of equipment, planning to transfer my mother from the house to the shop while she whisked her egg whites into snowy peaks. By the time she reached her new workplace she had made a bowl of meringue and was demanding we give her back her piping tube. She made pajaritos dulces, piping the meringue into roses, each one with a missing petal.

My father, who could just about manage his taxes, now saw himself in the difficult situation of running a business. At first, our only customers were his family and friends who visited out of pure loyalty, or, as was more likely, a secret curiosity to see for themselves if the rumors about my mother were true. But before the first week had passed, we began to see new faces. Most were mothers like my own, although the ages ranged from the very young, who were expecting new children, to the elderly, who had seen their own grow up into parents themselves. With each payment they would nod and send their blessings to my mother in an unspoken pact of solidarity. I didn't understand these women but they understood my mother.

The queue to get inside grew longer with each passing day, stretching past our door and onto the street, sometimes even turning into the corner so that you couldn't see the end if you stood at the entrance. We were now attracting all types of customers, from all backgrounds and ages. For the first time on this street, the rich had to stand next to the poor and forgotten as each one waited their turn to be served. By the time the first month was up we had earned enough to redecorate our shop as well as hire additional help at the till, although my mother would never allow anyone else to work in her kitchen. She spent her nights and days baking, never leaving her post and only sleeping on her feet an hour a night. My father and I begged her to rest, but it had been weeks since she acknowledged anything we said to her. The only time she would momentarily stop was to ask if we'd heard anything about Joaquin. Each time we'd say no she'd return to her work with a renewed fervor.

We knew that sooner or later we would have to serve one of the uniformed. It was inevitable: we were a booming pastry shop set up a few blocks away from the offices at the Edificio Diego Portales, where they all worked. Everyone knew they had a sweet tooth, that they liked to indulge their appetite. Yet it still surprised us that day when we saw that green uniform step through our door and bolt it shut. He made his way across the room to the counter, ignoring the line of customers that had been left inside. Leaning over the counter with a smug smile, he examined the pastries behind me. I could smell a sour hint of garlic on his breath.

"When they told me this was the best bakery in all of Chile I didn't expect to find someone so young running it," he said after slowly licking his lips.

"It's not mine, sir," I answered. "My mother is the one who bakes. Can I get you anything?"

He pursed his lips, making his moustache and chin all the more prominent.

"Mija, it's sergeant, not sir. And yes," he said looking behind me, "I'll have a piece of that milhojas."

My father who had seen everything from the other side of the shop joined me behind the counter.

He cut the sergeant a generous portion of the cake, much larger than what he would normally give.

"It's what they're used to," he whispered. "That's why they're all guatones."

Without moving to let other customers past, the sergeant ate his cake over the counter, spilling crumbs onto the work surface on our side. When he finished, he wiped his mouth with a tissue my father gave him, leaving a trace of manjar on the corner of his moustache.

"I'm not sure what I expected," he said giving my father back the empty plate with the crumpled tissue, "but I can say I am surprised.

Please send my regards to the chef, a truly remarkable woman. I can guarantee you'll be seeing a lot more of us now."

Without so much as a goodbye, he turned and strolled out, parting the line of customers that had watched everything in a sober silence. Before serving the next customer, my father made me swear I wouldn't tell my mother what had happened. I told him I wouldn't, knowing well that my mother always kept the kitchen door open anyway.

Despite the sergeant's promise, we didn't see another uniform in the shop until a couple of weeks after the first visit. Unlike the sergeant, the officer that came this time waited his turn in the line, listening nervously to the woman beside him who had a list of complaints regarding a security guard on her block. When he arrived at the counter, I noticed that instead of medals, his jacket was adorned with two sweat patches.

"I've come with an order from the offices at the Edificio Diego Portales requesting that the present bakery cease its deliveries of baked goods immediately we are thankful for the products you have continuously sent to us nonetheless as of today your services are no longer required nor welcomed," he said in one breath. I could tell from the way he squinted his eyes that he had been told to memorize and repeat the order word for word.

With a large grin on his face, my father reached for a berlin on the shelf behind him, wrapped it in a napkin and put it on the counter in front of the officer.

"Whilst my daughter and I would gladly respect such a request," he answered, "I must clarify that we haven't sent any cakes to the Edificio Diego Portales. And please," he gestured at the berlin on the counter, "help yourself to one of our specialties. On the house."

It took a few seconds for the officer to react. Confused, he picked up the berlin, looking from my father to the cake and back again. I noticed his upper lip had a thin moustache, no thicker than the one Joaquin had tried to grow before he disappeared.

"But you d-do," he finally stuttered. "Every day we receive hundreds of your cakes."

My father shook his head and shrugged his shoulders.

"Wherever you're getting them from, I can promise you they're not from here."

The young officer's eyebrows furrowed as he searched for a response. Unable to find the right words, he turned and left. We could see him through the shop window as he unwrapped the berlin and nibbled it, his face still distorted by the scowl that hadn't left. He didn't notice the bit of custard that fell onto his uniform.

Every day after that visit we would attend one of the uniformed. They each came with the same request, leaving with the same answer and a pastry which they invariably ate before they were out of sight. It became common knowledge that the men at the Edificio Diego Portales were struggling to contain the large volumes of cake they received every day. People described the way these desserts appeared in their filing cabinets or in their drawers, how it wasn't uncommon for an official to accidently sit on an empolvado and to be seen walking around with powdered sugar on his bottom. There had even been a rumor that because of a jam stain on a document, a police unit not too far from us had received an order of five hundred balloons instead of batons.

It wasn't long after this final incident that we saw a large military van pull up to the shop. Sensing something had changed, my mother emerged from the kitchen with a bowl in her arms. She was mixing the dough for a dozen tacitas. Through the shop window, the three of us watched as the military men opened the door and threw out one cake after another onto the street, as if they were bags of coal rather than carefully assembled pastries. Once they had emptied their cargo, they jumped back in the van and drove off, leaving the thick carpet of smashed desserts on the pavement that was already attracting nearby flies.

For the first time since Joaquin's disappearance, I saw my mother put down the mixing bowl. Without saying a word, she stormed out of the shop. My father and I followed closely behind, ordering one of the apprentices to watch the till while we were gone. There was no need for that though, as the line of customers that had been snaking into our shop soon followed my mother. At the pace she walked, it didn't take long for us to arrive at the Edificio Diego Portales, its glass structure looming over the crowd as we stood outside its main entrance. On the lawn in front of the building sat an assortment of pastries. The collection grew by the minute as officials coming in and out of the building deposited new desserts on the grass. Through the glass doors we could see the receptionist hiding behind the rows of cakes that had piled up on the desk's surface.

My mother picked up the nearest pastry, a pie de limón, and carried it into the reception, quickly leaving before the receptionist could say anything. She repeated the act, bringing back into the building the cakes the officials had left on the lawn, ignoring the receptionist's protests each time she entered the building. Bewildered, many of the officials who had been carrying cakes outside stood still, marveled by my mother's determination as she carried up to ten cakes at a time. None of them dared intervene, knowing well not to get in the way of a mother's anger. Finally, the youngest of the officers approached her. His uniform was cleaner and smoother than the others, perhaps being used for the first time. As my mother bent down to pick up a raspberry meringue cake, the officer tapped her on the shoulder, touching her so lightly that it took her a while to realize he was there.

"Señora," he said quietly, "what are you doing? Why don't you go home? This is no place for a woman like you."

My mother tightened her grip on the cake, her fingers digging into the pink meringue.

"I'll go when you tell me where my son is," she snarled.

"I'm sorry, I don't know who –"

"Joaquin," she spat. "Where is he?"

She threw the cake into his hands, covering his thin fingers in its pink sludge. Turning to a nearby officer she asked him the same question. He didn't answer. She looked for another officer, and then another, her voice growing louder each time she repeated the question.

"Where is he?" she cried.

Forty-five years later we're still asking the same question.

Elizabeth Jane

As well as a writer, Elizabeth Jane Corbett was a librarian, taught Welsh at the Melbourne Welsh Church, and was the Social Media Coordinator for the Historical Novel Society Australasia. She won the 2009 Bristol Short Story Prize (writing as Elizabeth Jane) and was shortlisted for the Allan Marshall Short Story Award. Her debut novel, *The Tides Between*, was named a Children's Book Council of Australia Notable Book for older readers. She liked red shoes, dark chocolate, commuter cycling, and reading quirky, character driven novels set once-upon-a-time in lands far away. Very sadly Liz passed away in early 2020.

BEYOND
THE BLACKOUT
CURTAIN

I had known something was wrong all day. Not the ordinary, wartime, kind of wrong, something oily and sinister like the fumes over Llandarcy oil works. The whole earth had trembled during the night. This morning we had scrambled blinking from our air-raid shelter, to find the sky smudged and grey. As I stood in the hallway, my fingers fumbling with the ribbons in my hair, I heard Davis the Dairy tell Mam things were bad over by Swansea.

I sat with my face to the living room fire and let its heat scorch my cheeks. Cosy it was with the embers shifting in the hearth and my sister Audrey curled up in the chair opposite. I heard Mam bustling about in the scullery. Dad would be home soon. It was my turn to set the table. But I hadn't started. I felt lazy all over, like a Guy Fawkes without straw, now that I knew Aunty Annie was safe.

The school day had been played out slowly. My mind was dull in

Composition. My thoughts had wandered during Mental Arithmetic. Time and again, I had worried about Aunty Annie. Had she made it to the air-raid shelter on time? Was Mrs Thomas, her landlady alright? What about her house on Teilo Crescent, with its oak dresser and Swansea china plates, was it all smashed to the ground?

It wasn't the first time Swansea had been bombed. I should have been used to it, but my second-hand concern had grown brand new since Aunty Annie married Sion Evans and went to live with him in Swansea.

Mam had made me toast, cut into soldiers. While she wasn't looking, I dipped them in my milk. The butter made little yellow oil spills on the surface. I leaned over the mug and slurped noisily. As if from afar, I heard my sister Audrey chiding.

'Stop slurping,' she said, laying her book down. 'And eat your toast properly.'

I took another loud sip and, still chewing the soggy toast, I grinned like an All-Hallows turnip.

'Mam,' Audrey yelled. 'Linda's annoying me.'

'Never mind Linda,' Mam called back. 'Come and make your Dad's tea.'

I heard my Mam's voice sharp as she told Audrey to spread the butter thinly, followed by the flare of a match, the bang of the kettle, and the hiss of water being poured. Mam had a mood like a nettle on her this evening. It surprised me. Normally it was all lightness and laughter with us, once we knew Aunty Annie was safe. We would have jam on our toast and sugar in our tea. Then, for a few days, we would live as if the bombers might never come again.

But tonight things were different. There was something Mam wasn't telling me. I had seen it in the tight smiles on the teachers' faces, the whisper of older students in the school yard. It was something about Swansea.

On a clear day, when I stood on the sand hills above Aberafan Beach, it felt like I could reach across the bay and touch Swansea. There were only four miles between Aberafan Sands and Swansea Docks (I had heard Rhys Price tell my sister Audrey). It took all morning to get to there by bus, mind. The route wound in and out of villages like a maze in my puzzle book.

The Germans weren't interested in Swansea Market or its bustling High Street. Dad said they wanted to damage the wharf and the chemical plant at Landore. For the same reason, only two nights ago, they had bombed Llandarcy oil works.

But sometimes the bombers missed their target. Then the bombs fell on the streets of the towns. That's why the military had put sandbags around the buildings in Aberafan with barrage balloons and barbed wire along the seashore. They had taken the stack down from on top of the *foel**, too, so the Germans wouldn't find our docks and steelworks. Night after night, when the sirens wailed, we would run to the air-raid shelter at the bottom of our garden, and pray for the bombers to pass.

The click of the front door pulled me from my thoughts. I heard my father's boots on the doorstep and felt the icy draft.

'Close the curtains,' he called out. 'Blackout's started.'

I scrambled to my feet.

'They'll not be coming tonight,' Mam said, emerging from the scullery. 'Llandarcy's a beacon. They'll be back to finish off Swansea.'

'Is it us that's making the rules, now?' he asked, brushing a kiss across her cheek.

Mam moved about the house closing the heavy curtains. I helped Dad shrug out of his coat and laid it on the back of the chair to dry.

The grey wool felt cold and damp in my hands, as if he had brought the winter inside.

'What's a beacon?' I asked, quietly.

My father turned slowly, his hand rising to the stubble on his chin. 'Well *bach**, you'll know where Llandarcy is?'

'Past Briton Ferry,' I said. 'On the way to Swansea.'

'Clever girl,' he smiled. 'What else can you tell me?'

'It's burning. I heard Rhys Price tell our Audrey.'

'Burning bright,' he said, no longer smiling. 'Like a crack in the curtains it is, see.'

I nodded, not trusting myself to speak. All day I had heard the whispers, had seen the teachers' anxious faces. I had smelled the thick black fumes coming from Llandarcy. But I had missed their message. I had thought, if only Aunty Annie were safe, my worries would be over. Now I knew they were just beginning.

After tea, Mam and Dad pulled their chairs up close to the fire. I sat at the living room table with my chin in my hands and stared blankly at my spelling list. Flickering firelight made patterns on the peony print wallpaper. Audrey's pencil scraped softly as she made neat columns in her work book. Mam and Dad talked about Aunty Annie, their voices rising and falling like the soft spread of an owl's tawny wings.

'If only there was something we could do,' Mam's fingers plucked at the pleats in her skirt.

'There's nothing,' Dad said, reaching out to squeeze her hand. 'Just keep ourselves safe.'

'I expect you're right,' Mam swallowed. 'But it feels cowardly hiding underground while my sister might be dying.'

Mam's words caught at the small dark fear lurking beneath my jersey and made my tummy twist. I didn't want Aunty Annie to die. She had

Mam's eyes and her same soft way of talking. She bought me sweets, sometimes, and Beano comics. My eyes prickled at the thought of her hurt and bleeding. I slithered from my chair and crawled beneath the table to where it was dark and hidden.

When I was younger, Mam would spread a rug out under the table, and I would play there for hours. It was my secret place, a safe place. My world apart from all that was happening. But today as I crept into my hidey-hole, I knew there would be no escaping. There was only a narrow space, between the tablecloth and the floor, but it made a ring of light on the carpet. If I closed my eyes, momentarily, I might pretend not to see it. But when I opened them, just a crack, the light filtered in. I could see Audrey's feet in her brown lace-up shoes and the scab on her knee. Bright it was, like a crack in the curtain, and all the while, like a chemist's lamp, Llandarcy was burning.

The siren came at around half past eight, its long thin wail sounding high with fright. From beneath the table I saw Mam and Dad rise. I scrambled out from my hiding place. Mam held my coat out for me as Audrey came back from the hallway carrying our scarves and hats. Dad had our papers bundled and ready like he always did. I heard shouts, the sound of doors banging up and down the street, and all the while the siren howled right through me.

We didn't go out through the back door. It was the first thing that puzzled me. Followed by the sight of Mam and Dad conferring, heads together, their voices like wind in the trees.

'You stay with the girls,' Mam said. 'I'll go by myself.'

'It's daft,' Dad shook his head. 'It won't change anything.'

I didn't understand the delay. Usually Mam and Dad were like coiled springs once the siren had sounded. After hours of waiting, movement brought relief. Bundled in our warmest clothes we would hurry down the path between rows of cauliflower and cabbage to the air-raid shelter at the bottom of our garden.

But tonight the front door-latch was lifted. Mam ushered us out onto the blackened street with a finger to her lips.

'Hold Audrey's hand,' she said, as we headed towards Villiers Street.

I tripped along the dark streets, my breath coming in soft cotton-wool clouds as I struggled to keep up.

'Where are we going?' I asked, as we turned right and followed Ynys Street down towards the centre of town.

'Never mind,' Audrey said. 'Just be quick.'

The night wore a blanket of silence now and, strangely, we weren't the only ones on the street. There were others gliding along in the shadows with their heads down and collars turned up against the wind. Like market day it was, except, the shops were dark and empty. Where were the wardens, I wondered, with their tin hats and their arm bands? We weren't allowed out during an air-raid. Dad knew that. His face was stern beneath his cloth cap. But Mam didn't look at him. She had her eyes fixed straight ahead.

We slipped down the High Street, turning left at Mayfield's Dairy, and carried on past the cemetery schools until we reached the tin-plate works. Then turning right we followed the curving road towards Sandfields.

Beautiful Aberafan was in the moonlight, with ice glistening on the tarmac and soft snowfall draped on the window sills and eaves. It seemed to me a fairy world all fragile and glistening. It was hard to believe anyone could drop a bomb on such a night. Yet I could hear the Luftwaffe approaching like a swarm of bees.

We didn't stay on the road, though it would have taken us all the way to the shore. Once we had passed the railway, we turned right and headed out across the sand hills, winding our way through hillocks and tufts of grass until we were overlooking the bay. Eerie it was, with the moon laying its silver tracks across the water and searchlights sweeping the sky. The wind came off the water in gusts, whipping my face. I closed my eyes, sniffing the salt spray, listening to the slush and boom of the sea.

We weren't alone on the sand hills. Minute by minute, others straggled over to join us. The Burdocks arrived first, followed by the Jenkins and Jones families. Then it was Mrs Prosser who hadn't spoken to Mrs Jones since their falling out at the Red Cross auxiliary. Ben Aaron arrived next (he always walked with a limp); followed by Glynis Owen, with her new baby bundled up against the wind.

After that it was like the Whitsun procession on Aberafan High Street. There were the O'Leary's, from St Joseph's, who had so many children Mam had stopped counting; and Boyo Howells, the butcher's boy, who always pulled faces at me. Old Mrs Lewis was there, too. Never mind that she was poorly. Even Sam the Dogs was there, though no one really liked him. Alone and in groups, people kept coming until, it seemed to me, the whole village was there on the sand, all watching and waiting.

The humming grew steadily louder as the sky filled with bombers. Like a flock of steel birds, they were, all flying in formation. Suddenly flares lit the night sky and hung there like lanterns. Then fire began to rain down on Swansea. From across the water, I heard the sound of distant fire-engines and the rattle of anti-aircraft guns.

The heavy bombs came next, in salvos of six. Their high-pitched whistle seemed to fill the night, jeering at us, as we stood huddled on the beach. I don't know how long we stood there, hours it seemed, with the night so bright I could have read my spelling list.

I saw the town, a paper cut-out against the horizon and the cranes on the docks like fingers reaching up into the heavens. But the bombs weren't hitting the docks. I could see that quite clearly. From St Thomas to Brynmill the suburbs were being bombarded. Beyond the town centre, where Aunty Annie and Sion Evans lived, there was a mighty roar, followed by spreading tongues of fire, like on Pentecost morning.

Beside me, I heard Dad trying to comfort Mam.

'She'll be alright,' he said, over and over. 'It's safe underground.'

Mam didn't believe him. Her face was pressed up hard against his chest, her shoulders shaking. As Audrey's hand found mine in the dark, I realised she too was crying.

Funny it is, while standing amid such sorrow, that you can detect a hint of change. Like the first shoot of daffodil poking through the winter's soil. One minute there's nothing and then, suddenly, a green tip breaks the earth, unbidden, while you are still warding off the season's chill. That's how it was with me, or so it seemed. For a long time there was nothing but fire and explosions, long low shrills and the sound of people sobbing. Then from behind me, all soft and unimposing, came the pitch of a man's voice. I turned, trying to catch its echo, and saw it came from the mouth of old Dai Hopkins.

My Dad told me, when Dai Hopkins was a young man it would bring tears to your eyes to hear him sing. He wasn't young anymore. His voice was spidery thin. But he still knew how to pitch a note. He stood with his eyes closed and his hair all silver in the moonlight, and began to raise the singing.

Mae hen wlad fy nhadau yn annwyl i mi,
The old land of my fathers is so dear to me ...

Like a pointer dog I was, with the hair on the back of my neck rising and the breath catching in my throat and my eyes prickling.

Gwlad beirdd a chantorion, enwogion o fri,
Land of poets and singers, famous men of renown …

His voice wasn't loud. Old Dai Hopkins was too frail to sing forcefully. But as he sang, one by one, others began to join him.

Ei gwrol ryfelwyr, gwladgarwyr tra mâd,
Her brave warriors, very splendid patriots …

Powerful it was, like the Severn Bore, a great tidal wave rolling and swelling against the river's course. Men raised their heads and squared their shoulders. Women stood with flushed cheeks, their eyes strangely defiant. Their babies hushed, no longer crying.

I turned and, out of the corner of my eye, saw Mrs Prosser nod stiffly to Mrs Jones. I heard Ben Aaron and Patrick O'Leary singing harmonies with the vicar from St Agnes. Then, like a seam of coal riven from its mountain fastness, I heard Dad's voice ring out.

Dros ryddid collasant eu gwaed,
For freedom shed their blood …

My breath came in hard, chest aching gulps as I sought Mam's arms. She turned, blinded by Swansea's smoke, and reached out to gather me. Her embrace was lavender and talcum powder, amid those choking fumes. Her voice was her own, yet so much like Aunty Annie's. Her singing low and tremulous, as her work-roughened hand stroked my cheek.

And in that moment, as I stood in the shadow of those grim fireworks, with the sea before me, and the mountains behind, and the people of my village singing, it seemed that old Dai Hopkins was a harpist and we his harp strings – all vibrant and lovely and quivering. Then I too raised my voice and sang for Aunty Annie and Sion Evans, and the many others who died that night in Swansea.

Rebecca Lloyd

Apart from short stories in anthologies, Rebecca Lloyd's work includes four short story collections, four novels, and two novellas. Some of her short stories have been reprinted by Salt Publishing, PS Publishing and Night Shade Books. Her recent work includes *The Child Cephalina*, a Gothic novel published by Tartarus Press in 2019, *The Bellboy*, published by Zagava in 2018, and *Woolfy and Scrapo*, a novella, published by Zagava in 2023. Literary awards in which she has been acknowledged include The World Fantasy Award, the 2008 Bristol Short Story Prize, the Aestas Short Story Prize, the Paul Bowles Short Fiction Award and the Screencraft Cinematic Short Story Contest. Details of much of her work can be found at www.beccalloyd.org

THE RIVER

I didn't know my grandfather had started fishing again until the landlord of *The Ropemaker* beckoned me one afternoon as I came home from work. 'I've banned him from the walkway. You should look after him better, Miss,' he warned me. 'He pulled up a whopper and my son had to help him with it. They lost it. The old geezer said he'd gladly have gone down with it.'

'Sounds like him,' I said. 'How big?'

'Girth of a drainpipe, apparently.'

Grandpa was on the balcony as I came in, looking down at the floating rubbish island that docked for a short while between our house and *The Ropemaker*. 'We never had rubbish like this at Tilbury,' he said.

'It's all the trash from the city, Grandpa.'

'Where do you think it goes?'

'Down to the sea, I expect. You were fishing again. You said you were done with it all.'

'Tide's coming in fast, look.'

At high tide, water slapped across our balcony floor and wetted the windows. In violent weather, you could feel its force as it struck the house wall below, and pulled away and struck again. There was a drop of twenty-five feet between tides, and at low tide, the foreshore was exposed for as far as we could see in either direction. We liked the sound of the river's brown waves rolling upwards as the tide came in again, they made the pebbles gleam, and deposited their foamy edges in a ridge of scum as they reached out again for the river walls.

'Next door said you were fishing.'

'I was just checking that there really are big fish up here so close to the city. That kid from the pub had an eel bucket. I was curious.'

I'd forgotten the long hours my grandfather spent alone. I stared at the scores of plastic milk bottles moving serenely amongst the rubbish. 'Did you eat something?'

'Couldn't open the biscuit packet. Could no more open the bloody thing than get out of my own coffin,' he muttered.

Grandpa used to dream about his death. I'd glimpse him sometimes through the patchy mirror above the stove when we got up in the morning, and terror was clear on his face. 'You can warp a persistent bad dream,' I'd told him. 'If you think about it angrily, you can take your anger back into the dream and change the course of it.'

'Is that so, Maggie?'

'Try it with the dreams you have. Tell yourself you just have to reach your hands up and push the lid off, and in a minute you'll be out and free.'

'Tell myself I'm not on fire alone in a dark place amid horrible music?'

'Tell yourself that before the coffin slides behind that creepy curtain that doesn't even sway, you burst out and run through the crematorium, laughing.'

'That'd be funny,' he said, but I could hear him thinking it wouldn't make a jot of difference to the real thing. He pretended it was working for a while; inventing moments in his dreams I suspected weren't true,

'I was flying above Tilbury and I could see the river below me, all glinting in the sun.'

'Yeah?'

'It was glorious. I flew in the vaults of the church and I could see figures below with their hands raised up, and they were all hissing with anger. Then I flew over our old house with the concrete yard and the outside toilet.'

'Really? But, Grandpa, when you die, you're free from that very moment. You don't know anything then.'

'Maggie, it's not deadness itself, it's how they fiddle and fuss, and what they do to you; they take away a man's uniqueness.'

'But you won't know.'

'I will. I know now, unless you can do something about it for me.'

I'd had a persistent dark dream about his death as well, one I didn't tell him about for fear he'd covet it. I sing in the dream desperately, but it makes no difference, the monster he caught when I was seven slithers off the bank with scarcely a ripple, taking him under the brown water with it.

I never did go down to the river with him again after the day he landed the creature, and a while ago he told me he'd regretted me being there too, 'It was a man to man thing, and you were only a wee girl.'

The smaller eels, bootlaces he called them, weighed only a few pounds, and when they wrapped themselves around his wrists like living bracelets, I'd thought it funny. My job was to make a groove in the earth by the bank. 'A bed for them,' he said, 'so they're all comfy when we get them up.'

When the big hit came, Grandpa got to his feet very quickly. I saw him brace his legs and straighten his back. He whistled low under his breath and muttered something. He gave no slack on the line, and three times the great eel headed fast for the rushes and he forced it out into the open again. 'Make the bed really big,' he called to me. I could feel my heart thumping against my knee as I scraped at the soft mud with my trowel. 'Make another groove through the middle so it's like a cross. Do it quick, Maggie.'

The backs of Grandpa's legs were trembling. He had the net ready, and the eel was close to it. It rose to the surface and thrashed its pointed head about, fighting hard and foaming up the water. Five times he nearly lost it, then, when he finally brought it to the bank, the fight between them escalated. Grandpa shouted and pleaded with the thing in turns. It thwacked violently in his grip and I thought he'd fall into the water with it. I backed away and looked towards the path, thinking to run home and hide.

Finally, he had it tight in both hands, holding it at arm's length, upside down. It was thicker than a lamppost, a great slimy pillar of silver-grey muscle. It seemed a long while before Grandpa moved again to lay it in the groove on its back. He beckoned me to crouch down beside him, and taking my trembling hand, showed me how to stroke it so it'd stay quiet. 'Talk to it, Maggie. Stroke it softly.'

I felt like crying. 'What'll I say, Grandpa?'

'Sing the hymn you learnt in school last week.'

'All Things Bright And Beautiful'?

'That's it. I've got to ease the hook out, and the man must stay very still so I don't harm him.'

I remember the sound of my thin voice singing on the wrong note, and the feel of my fingertips on the slime of the eel's belly. It wasn't deep-hooked and Grandpa was glad. 'See, Maggie,' he said, as he watched me work the creature, 'you don't have to be strong, or a man, to do something awesome in life.'

And that was it; that was, the feeling that had come upon me, if awe is a solemn quiet thing that reaches deep inside you.

'Why do you throw the big ones back, Grandpa?'

'Because they've come so far against the odds; three thousand miles from the Sargasso Sea. Mind you, no one's ever found an eel egg there.' He took the hook gently out of the animal's lip. 'This man's a toothy one, see? That means he hunts fish, and doesn't bother much with bloodworms and things.' He scooped the beast into his arms, and cradling it there for a moment, took it to the river's edge. As it slithered off the muddy bank and away into the water, I wiped my slimy fingers on my dress and Grandpa waved to it.

'I'm glad he's back, he looked all wrong out of the water.'

'Oh, you'd be surprised the places you find eels, and how far they can travel over land. They're gypsies. They're clever and free, not tied down like most people are, you know.'

On the night of the eclipse of the moon, I took the old armchair out of the living room and onto the balcony, and settled my grandfather in it with a blanket. 'A good night for eels,' he said.

'Grandpa, you remember when we got the big one, Why did I have to make two grooves for it?'

'Oh, I just got over excited. My own grandfather always made a cross for eels to get the devil out of them. They're not like other fish, they get anywhere where there's water.'

I remembered the great wriggling mass of muscle and the way Grandpa sighed when he took the hook out of its lip. 'How big do you reckon it was?'

'He must have had a twelve-inch girth, and I had him at about four foot. I've always wished I'd caught him at night. There's nothing like eel fishing in the moonlight. They go into the upper layers of water and the moon makes the small fish visible to them. You use a float then, and they're a sight to see swirling around the bait before they take it.'

'Did you do that Grandpa, fish at night?'

'Of course I did. They're nocturnal feeders, those men.'

'While I was asleep at home?'

He shrugged. 'Yes, sometimes.'

'Did you want to be free – like an eel?'

He laughed. 'Who wouldn't?'

'You left me at home. How often?'

'Oh, things were safe in those days, my love. It's not like now.'

'What is now like, Grandpa?'

He rocked forward for a moment and slumped back in his chair. I kept my eyes on the moon; it was brilliantly silver with grey countries all over it. 'It's meaner, Maggie, darker. When you get old, you can't be bothered with meanness and darkness because it's not your time anymore. But you don't want to mention it, because the ones you love, in my case the single one, have to go on living in it.'

My throat tightened. 'Was I a burden to you all those years after Mum and Dad died?'

'Don't be daft, Girl, you were the centre of everything for me, you and the men.'

'How often did you go out at night?'

'Well, you came with me at the weekends, didn't you? You seemed to enjoy it before I caught the big one. You were all queer and dreamy on the way home that day. I felt as if I didn't know who you were.'

'I sometimes feel as if I don't know you. How often?'

'Every night,' he whispered. 'Came back at dawn. There now.'

'Christ, Grandpa!'

'It's in my blood Maggie, eel fishing. I could never resist it.'

'Every night. I was a burden to you then.'

'It's hard bringing up a kid, Maggie. But you were no burden, not like I am to you now.'

'You're not, Grandpa. Don't think that.'

'Thank you, Maggie. But I've become a burden to myself.'

The moon was changing colour, dimming to a strange browny-red, and by the time we went inside it was hanging in the sky like a moist red grape.

The rubbish island came our way on the high tide at around four o'clock. The larger objects, lumps of polystyrene and wooden planks, gave the thing cohesion, between them floated plastic bottles of all kinds, and the lids from take-away cappuccinos. I never saw an island without a couple of footballs amongst the jumble, and a few shoes. The whole sad flotilla, a peculiar combination of the once cared-for and the utterly irrelevant, stayed together in the calm waters, and if disrupted by a wave thrown up suddenly by a speeding boat, formed as one mass again quickly, aided by the underwater currents.

It was as if each object, disengaged from its original purpose, found a new legitimacy in the great river, where in its kinship with other floating things it formed a forlorn mosaic about the lives of careless people. And objects that once had meaning, private things – shoes, baseball caps, the occasional jacket, gave the island a curious poignancy as they floated amongst the other trash.

'Why are you taking pictures of it, Maggie?'

I'd rather Grandpa had thought my work was to do with the light and the sky; I didn't think he'd understand my fascination with ordinary things in the wrong places. 'There's interesting stuff down there, Grandpa.'

He came to stand beside me. 'I suppose there is. Are people going to buy pictures of sunglasses and rubber sandals all bobbing and floating in the water like that?'

'I don't know yet.'

'Funny business, life.'

He became ill for a couple of weeks that spring and the last of his stamina and muscle fell away from him. I stayed at home and sat with him on the balcony. We played a game of trying to name the colours on the river before they changed. There were afternoons when the tiny choppy waves that signalled the incoming tide were yellow ochre at their crests in the low sunlight, and the writhing valleys of water between them were a war of deep blue and silver. Yet, you could turn away for a second and look again to find the waves had dulled to a translucent muddy brown, and the green algae on the river wall was no longer vivid.

He was as light as a cuttlefish bone, and I could've carried him easily through the rooms of the house if he'd allowed it. Instead, he shuffled painfully from one room to the other and out onto the balcony. It was fine weather. In the early morning, a silvery-blue light lay across the metal roofs of the factories on the other side of the river so they looked like slabs of molten metal, and the detail on all the buildings was obliterated in the haze so they became no more than giant cubes.

I took him out to walk on the foreshore at low tide, along the band of white sand against the river wall. Closer to the edge of the water the sand turned to fine grey silt dotted with half bricks from houses once standing along the shore. We could smell the sea the Thames finally reaches sometimes, and in the sunlight, the old bricks cast square shadows behind them on the wet mud.

Then quite suddenly one morning, my grandfather was gone. I checked the street and the local store. I called out for him stupidly, and finally went to *The Ropemaker*. The landlord hadn't seen him and he looked at me distantly and hopelessly.

At four o'clock that day, the son walked in through my open door and joined me on the balcony. 'No luck yet?' I shook my head. I'd fallen into a terrible dreaming state, a state of knowing and denying at the same time. Of all the people I might've wanted with me, this ugly youth with remote eyes that slid about and never rested, was not one.

The island submerged and surfaced languidly, pale. Two tennis balls, furry and light green, bobbed amongst the rubbish and a shoe floated sole upwards nearby. I noticed the second shoe emerge from beneath a slab of polystyrene, and as if by its own effort, turn itself over to mimic its partner. The water was dark, all its facets sombre, slate-grey and rippling. A shaft of sudden sunlight flung a field of silver across its surface and blurred the island's contents. No boats mangled the pattern of currents and ripples, no birds flew overhead. A plastic paint bucket, half sunk and half floating, moved amongst the sticks and bottles. As the sun dimmed, a face appeared within the island, a face and body, hands waxen.

The boy caught hold of my arm and I didn't pull away. 'It'll go down to the sea presently,' he murmured.

He was beautiful down there; the water had softened the sharp contours of his face, and his hair floated around him like fine weed. His hands were relaxed and his fingers spread open as if in a gesture of welcome. He'd put on his navy-blue suit, and his tie lay like a strap around his chin. One of his shoes had come off, and he hadn't bothered to put on any socks. A sodden trilby floated nearby with a feather in the headband, it wasn't Grandpa's, but he would've liked it.

'There was an old geezer in the water a couple of years ago,' the boy whispered, 'in the lower pool by Wapping.' I began to cry. 'Only in his case he didn't have no family. He had a purse on him, they said, and they found a note in it written in grammar. It said I am Shaun Peters. I have no relations.

'To my way of thinking Jimmy was a lucky man having you.' He let go of my arm and shuffled backwards as if he'd suddenly become aware of his intimacy with me.

The island began to creep out of the recess inch by inch as the currents changed. Grandpa floated in the midst of it, elegantly. I could feel my fingers bruising on the wooden rail. 'I don't know what to do.'

'Don't do nothing, Miss. He might make it to the open sea.'

I felt a sudden twist of anger. 'You didn't know my grandfather.'

'I did too. Him and me fished together most every afternoon.' His eyes were deep and steady, and on my face. 'He's me, only old. Don't disturb him now. He wants it this way. Look at him down there; it's like he's sleeping.'

The island swayed gently on its outward journey and Grandpa lay languid in the midst of it, and as I watched the beautiful serenity of the floating trash, I felt awe, if awe is a solemn quiet kind of thing that reaches deep inside you.

Paul McMichael

Paul McMichael was born along the rugged coast of Ireland's north-eastern corner, and now lives in London where he is married to Marc, his partner of 36 years. He has a career in electronics under his belt and so was late to catch the writing bug. He is a proud winner of the 2013 Bristol Short Story Award. Another story, *After the Rhododendrons* was short-listed for the Frank MacManus Prize 2013 and broadcast on Irish radio. Other stories have been long – or short-listed for the Fish Publications Prize, the Bath Award and the Brighton Prize. He has attended creative writing courses over the last few years and is working on his first novel, a coming-of-age quest and gay romance set in 1580 (fake news and hate speech have very long pedigrees).

THE HOUSE ON ST. JOHN'S AVENUE

(A short tale about love, family and theoretical cosmology)

I.

Eric and Jack have a dinner invite. Robert and Felipe have remodelled. There is mention of plantains. Something is bugging Robert.

We drive up and down three or four times, bickering about who should have gotten the full address from Robert. "I thought you had the number," says Jack. "You're maps and directions," I say.

"You're the keeper of the diary," Jack says. I scan to the left. "It's got to be that one." Georgian, steps to the side up to the raised ground floor, black panelled front door. Grand sash windows, two eyes on a lop-sided grin.

"Look at the fronds on that palm," Jack says.

"That'll be Felipe." I put a hand to Jack's arm. "Can you imagine the fuss at the garden centre?"

Jack puts on his not-very-Costa Rican accent. "Is very nice. But I need more big. Like Amazon."

Some kind of jungle envy thing.

We joke about how we'll force our jaws to the floor for the whole of the obligatory tour, exclaiming 'fabulous'. We do a five-point turn in the road and park. In the porch, tea lights in blown glass holders. We ring the bell. No one answers so we ring again. A pause before Felipe answers. Robert appears behind, looking sheepish. Then it's smiles, kiss, kiss, drinks, olives, nibbles, drinks. The wine is a Puligny-Montrachet 1997. "Monstruoso," Felipe says. It clings to the side like it wants to get out and join us for dinner.

Robert pours, the wine washing into each large balloon glass and sinking into a slow, buttery vortex. We bend our snouts to the trough.

Robert is tense. I try to get him on his own to find out more or to lend an ear. "Do you need a hand with dinner ?" I say.

"No, no, all under control," he says.

We bought them a shiny digital kitchen timer from Divertimenti. We might as well have flown by in an airship with the slogan, 'It's not about cooking, it's about timing'. The hosts fuss around in the kitchen.

I say, "Jack. Guess. Contemporary modern or Costa Rican fusion." Jack is trying to tune in to the sounds from inside. I go on. "I mean, access to half the world's flora and fauna in the rainforest, and yet a diet of plantains. Just, why?"

Jack laughs a little. He lays down a blanket of shhhs and pats it into place with his hand.

"I don't trust a fruit that versatile," I say. Jack laughs again.

Rumbling from the kitchen, terse voices. We slink down into the comfy sofa and hug our drinks.

We've known Felipe for about twelve years, since he first qualified at

St Barts. He was on-off with Alex at the time. It was Felipe's first big relationship.

I called him Callous Alex. Alex kept the Rolex.

Then there was Nate, the theatre nurse at the Clinic. Not the first coupling forged over medical grade steel but it ended badly. It turns out there were other eyes trained on Nate. Felipe got drunk and passed out on our couch. There were a few others, fleeting. Then one weekend in Brighton he met Robert. It seemed unlikely. A plastic surgeon. A barman. "Six months," said Jack, "seven if he's lucky."

"The first sunny day." I said.

But Robert moved quickly and firmly from one domain of being in the world to quite another and now it's been seven years and Jack and I are absolutely and completely chuffed for both of them.

Felipe is at the door with Robert.

"We do tour of the house," he says.

All very formal. That our approval should mean something feels good.

"Lovely. Dying to see what you've done," says Jack. Robert goes to top up the wine. Jack raises a hand to his glass. "Driving."

The tour starts. Their new place is lovely, a restrained period restoration. Jack and I are a bit jealous: downstairs, all light and grace; bathroom, serenity floor to ceiling; storage space, walk-through to master bedroom (the bastards).

Felipe shuffles on the stairs. Up or down? Is there more or is it back to the dining room? I see Robert thrum the fingers of both hands against the legs of his jeans.

"What's in here?" says Jack from the rear of the party. A closed door on the other side of the master bedroom.

Felipe steals a glance at Robert. "Oh... is nada," he says, his eyes flickering to Robert.

I knew it. What's in that room. I'm dying.

"Let's show them," says Robert.

Felipe hesitates then thunders back up to the landing. He jiggles Robert's arm. "Not now. Is not so good, come down, let's have dinner, yes?" Robert is unmoved.

II.
Secrets unveiled. A startling moment involving a cuddly toy.
Eric takes up novelty swearing.

Robert wrings his hands for a moment. "We said we would tell them," he says to Felipe. "I can't keep it a secret any longer." He approaches the door.

I feel like a nervous Alice before the rabbit hole. The door cracks, pastel blue walls inside. Another few inches. "A nursery!" I clamp a hand to my mouth. I look at Robert then back to the room. "Oh. My. God, you're pregnant! A baby. Wow, guys, a baby. Jack, we'll be uncles."

Jack says, "That's wonderful, Felipe, Robert, fantastic."

The room is almost ready, a step-ladder rests against a tall unit in the corner. I'm happy for them. "When is it, when is the big day?" I look at the two of them. Smiles of a kind, but not the unruly grins that say 'we're going to be dads'. There must be something else. Maybe there was a miscarriage. That would be terrible news. Then it comes to me. "Twins, no way. You're having twins!" I start a little up and down dance. I go to Felipe. "Is it yours?" I swivel. "Robert's?" I float off-piste on the wine. "No, no, I know, one of each!"

"Eric" says Jack.

Jack can say no with his eyebrows so I'm silenced.

"Not twins," says Felipe, "but sí, we are going to have a baby."

Then why so serious?

Robert goes on. "We didn't want to say before…."

Jack says, "So... how... where."

"America," says Robert. "Surrogacy."

"Is everything okay? So far?" Thoughtful Jack. One step ahead of me. They might not have wombs but they'll be worried and the poor woman is thousands of miles away.

"Muy bien," says Felipe, "with the baby, todo muy bien."

"Whose... you know... which of you…," says Jack.

He means who jizzed. Everyone's first question. It stands to reason. There is an egg and there is a sperm and that makes the donors the mum and the dad. The biological ones. Except they're not *Mum* and *Dad*, though it's mostly *Mum* in parenthood, isn't it? It was with mine, bless her grey hairs.

So here we have an egg, a borrowed womb. Mums? Dad and Dad? I raise my glass to the bold purpose of it all.

Felipe speaks. "We wait to find Latino egg donor. Rosa. She is from Arizona but la familia is Costa Rica."

So now we know the *how* and the *where*, but who jizzed? I think, that must be the reason for the tension between them now. Maybe since the baby is doing well, Robert regrets letting Felipe be the father. Maybe he dreads the first time they will go Costa Rica and have the arms of Mamá Figueres clutch her grandchild and whisper in Spanish about how her little man is going to grow up big and strong like his grandfather and 'is he on solids yet' and 'does he like plantains' and 'tell your *special friend* he can sleep in the spare room'.

Maybe I'm reading too much into this.

Felipe moves, looks askance at Robert. "There is some… thing." He searches Robert's face. There's high price to that look.

"Something?" Jack says.

"Not something. A thing," says Robert.

"A thing?" I say.

"It's an opportunity too, Felipe," says Robert.

My mind is a swirl. A giant baby? Disasters medical, legal, financial present themselves.

"You need to see it really," says Robert. He turns to Felipe. "I'll go down to the kitchen. What are you going to use?"

Felipe looks around, picks a grey and white rabbit from the chest of drawers. "Softie" he says.

Robert bounds to the door, leaps the stairs. He shouts up, "Ready!" He's in the kitchen I think, just below us.

Felipe takes the stepladder and places it near the corner of the room. He looks up then nudges the back feet an inch or two here and there. He goes to the brushed chrome panel by the door and touches one of the controls. Light floods the room. He mounts the steps and stretches out an arm. "Just watch," he says. For a moment he holds the toy by the feet, its toothy smile inverted to a rictus grin. He lets go.

The evening splits, a before and an after. I hear myself sniggering during the rabbit's fall toward the deep-pile crush of the carefully considered mid-blue carpet. I imagine Jack's verbal dismay at the build-up to the cheap laugh at our expense. But, as the rain slants inwards to lash the window panes, and with a quickening March wind asking to be let in to the warmth at the house on St. John's Avenue, the rabbit disappears.

Just disappears. Mid-fall. Gone.

"Fuck," says Jack.

Understated.

In words passed through the vortex of shock and mediated by the leviathan Puligny-Montrachet 1997, I clasp a hand to my forehead. "Holy Fuckness, Felipe. Holy Mother Fuckness."

III.

Robert pulls a rabbit out of the extra-dimensional space-time discontinuity. He is eager to explore, Felipe less so. Jack is sober, Eric less so. There is mention of plantains.

Robert appears at the door. He's holding Flopsy Wopsy. "Tah dah! We found the wormhole after the renovations," he says. "It goes through to the kitchen."

Felipe sits on the ladder's last step rubbing his head as if the whole thing hurts.

"A wormhole?" I say.

Robert goes on. "It's like a virtual fireman's pole. But in another dimension."

"I want one," I say, "Jack, get me one."

"Eric, we live on the ground floor."

"Robert, he never gets me anything," I say. "Did I tell you he got himself new clubs? Said he would go to the golf range and it would be good for his back. Hasn't been once since then. A fickle man." I raise my glass in Jack's direction.

"Who's been with the same guy for thirteen years," says Jack.

He's right. It's sweet. I'm now a little drunk.

"Those clubs are on eBay tomorrow," I say to Robert.

Robert tries to re-impose himself. "Listen, guys, listen. It could be the most important scientific discovery since… all the other discoveries humans have ever made put together!"

"We need one of those all-night theoretical cosmologists," I say.

Jack peers up at the point in mid-air where Flopsy vanished. "So how does this work then, Robert?"

Ergo, Robert is just a barman who doesn't know what he's talking about. I make a mental note: teach Jack about the line of grace between smart and supercilious.

Robert looks like he has a ping-pong ball in his mouth, huffing and puffing to pop it out as they do on those record breaker shows. He glances at Felipe from the tail of his eye. "There's something else we didn't tell you either."

Felipe steps off the ladder. "Robert–."

"We may as well tell them that too." Robert is on a roll. "Give me your phone Eric. I won't break it or anything, promise."

I place my shiny black slab of joy into his palm. "Better not."

"Right, I'll go down and catch it. You'll need to come with me to prove this Eric. Jack, when I shout, drop it through." He turns to Felipe, who is scowling from the ladder. "Oh, Felipe, please, don't be all sulky. It's going to be great. This is amazing. We're going to be rich."

Give or take an apartment in the south of France, they are plastic surgeon rich. Felipe keeps telling me he'll do any bits of me I'm not happy with. No thanks, my bits are fine. He also tells Jack he'll do any bits of me that Jack's not happy with. I let it go.

Robert and I head downstairs. He fetches the laundry basket from the utility room.

"Ready!"

I try to focus on mid-air but my eyes swim. I miss the phone reappearing. It thwumps from nowhere to the bottom of the wicker container. I fish it out from amongst the thick towels and tailored shirts. The front screen slides opens. It seems okay.

"Look at the date," says Robert.

I scroll. I look at Robert and smile. The date is last week. A short cut to the kitchen, and a time machine.

"Have I lost anything?" I scroll through. "Shit. Emails. I want a share of the profits for that. Ten per cent should cover it."

"Sorry," says Robert. "I forgot. Got a bit carried away."

"Robert." Felipe is at the door. "Let's discuss it, yes?" he says.

IV.

A delightful dinner. A discussion about the breach in the fabric of the universe. Plantains are consumed. Robert and Felipe argue. Eric and Jack are ringside.

Jack and I are hustled to the dining room. The papered walls and moulded ceiling puddle with the honeyed glow of big church candles. The silverware and glasses on the table are lined up like a parade of soldiers. A salad of figs and young Pecorino cheese, then leg of lamb, a kind of tagine, but with plantains (I knew it). Robert carries in a large dish, more of a small sailing vessel, brimming with impossibly green broccoli florets and French beans. "Sesame and truffle dressing," he says. Strictly no carbs but stuff yourself with everything else.

We do.

We push ourselves back from the table and stretch out.

Robert brings in a bottle of chilled Limoncello and three small glasses on a lacquered tray. I pour then lick the underside of my glass.

"Enough," says Jack.

"Me too," I say.

Robert talks excitedly about the space-time breach, its time travel possibilities. He's blethering on about human-kind's great scientific adventure at a new frontier. "It's safe for humans," he says. "I tried it first with a plantain. It *un-ripened*."

"I grew up on this fruit," Felipe says, "but I don't put my life in its hands."

I find that he does but I let it pass.

Robert places two hands in front of him. He thunders down the table. "And then I passed my saliva through the portal and sent it off for analysis." He looks around. "No change to my DNA. It still came out Anglo-Saxon. And possibly a little bit of Ghenghis Khan."

"That comes up a lot apparently," I say. Jack elbows me in the ribs.

"Very resourceful Robert," says Felipe, "but this proves nothing in medical terms. Gene mutation, epigenetics? You want to take such risks? With our baby coming?" He looks around at us. "Jack?"

"Robert, I think you're being naive," says Jack. "This isn't just about getting in the high-rolling risk takers looking for a cheap thrill. You'll have the council asking if we have a licence. The boffins will wrap the place in tin foil. The neighbours will resent you having a breach in the fabric of the universe in your house where they don't. There'll be soldiers in the front garden."

I sit up. "Soldiers?"

"In your dreams" says Jack. He eases the glass from my hands.

Felipe speaks again. "There will be a thousand cameras. Social services taking away the baby"

I bite my lips. Robert's face darkens, a low-pressure weather front moves north from the line of his lips.

"It's not just the money, Jack. And it's not just about celebrity, Felipe. Think what this could to do." He waits for a reply. "The terminally ill. We can help people. Maybe even cure them." He looks at Felipe. "Isn't that worth trying? We can do a good thing, it doesn't have to be just 'elective' time travel for the rich."

"I know such things as difference from elective to emergency," says Felipe.

True. A plastic surgeon makes his money in knowing just that. In the pause, I have time to look around the table. The ease and the banter have drained from the evening. The limoncello is out of reach and warming fast.

V.
Robert and Felipe take the argument for a tour of the house.
A time for honesty. Eric and Jack are transfixed.
Things end. Other things begin.

Felipe stands. "Robert, this is not about saving the world, is it? I remember you called me at the clinic. Remember? 'The egg has taken' you said, 'baby is growing'. But I see it in your eyes, you are less happy each day than the last."

No answer from Robert.

Felipe puts his shoulder to the point. "Is it my fault which embryos were stronger? 'More viable'. We agreed to it."

Robert squirms. He doesn't speak but there's a war inside him.

Jack rises from the chair. He says, "Er, we need to get up early so...."
I rise too.

"Please, don't go," says Felipe. "You should stay. Drink." He waves us back into our seats.

I reach for the limoncello but Jack moves the bottle another inch beyond the tips of my fingers. He's mean.

Felipe turns to Robert. "Robbie. I'm telling you, forget this stupid... wormhole? It is trouble. I see nothing but blue flashing lights."

"This isn't all about me. How is it that these Central Americans can be so macho sometimes and yet they're all big Mamá's boys at heart? You want to show *Mamacita* that even if you are the gay son who ran away to London, you can still father a child. Mamá will be so pleased, won't she? 'Come home to your real family. Let Mamá help you bring up your little Inca warrior'."

Robert starts stacking plates. Cutlery goes flying. I worry about the china. The two of them move to the kitchen sniping about Mamá and embryos with varying degrees of recrimination. Jack and I turn to the other door. Robert and Felipe go past and up the stairs.

I turn to Jack. He says, "Eric, we should go home."

"I know." I put on my sympathetic face. "But I'm not leaving before the end of the show."

It's not a play in one act. After an age, an epoch, I go the door and cock my ears to the drowned cadence of the voices upstairs.

Jack comes over. We take a tiny step into the hall, daring to gaze up, as if the sound will float down like leaves to catch on our upturned faces. Robert and Felipe are on the landing again. I mouth *nursery* to Jack. He screws up his face. I mime cradling. He puts a finger to my lips and nods. I take hold of Jack's hand.

The sniping has stopped. Their tone is softer now, cotton in the place of stone. Felipe is talking. "Yes I admit it, I do want to take baby to show Mamá. Soon. You know she won't come to London to this house. But I need you to be there. She needs to see we are a family now, that you are not just my *friend*. We are not going anywhere. I'm going to be so proud of you and the baby. I could not go without you."

"I guess I didn't say what I really felt. You talked so much about going back and Mamá and then it was your sperm that fertilised Rosa's Latino egg and… I just felt myself shut out of everything, that you didn't really need me."

"Robbie. Look around you. See? My life is all about us. This, we bought in Amsterdam, you loved it so much this painting. Those big white stones in the bathroom, I picked them from the beach where we met for our first anniversary. You said I am mad. And this, we argue so much about damn light switches in the shop you wouldn't let me in the car and it's raining and then we are laughing and I am so crazy to kill you. All these things we have, Robbie, they are pinning me down, in the heart, here."

In the hall, Jack and I try to live without oxygen for a moment.

"Our children, they should have all this in their hearts too. But this space-time... elevator thing, it will take all away, destroy our world. Their home too."

"Their home?" says Robert.

"Why not? We have frozen eggs, you have sperm, we will make another little one if Rosa will help us, half Costa Rican and half English... and a little bit Ghenghis Khan. And they will need two of us Robbie, it will not be so easy for our family sometimes."

Jack and I make faces. We do a silent victory jig and threaten to push each other over onto the restored and highly polished wooden floor and reveal ourselves. I don't know why. Jack is sober. We stop and listen again. A low growl, a kind of whimper above us. I know that sound, the animal note a man makes when he buries his face in the soft curve of another's neck. I know that sound.

Jack and I scamper back to the dining room when Robert and Felipe stir upstairs. We clatter into our seats and carry on the second half of a conversation that never started. The two of them come in, apologising. Felipe fetches in a bottle of whisky, says it's a special moment. They tell us they will try for Robert's baby with the surrogate, lovely Rosa from Arizona.

"What about your hole?" I say. They stare at me.

I point up. "The breach in the fabric of the universe?"

"Well, no invites to the world's press tonight," says Robert. He looks at his husband. He takes Felipe's hand. "I was wrong. It's all about the baby now. So… we'll lower the ceiling or have it built in. Maybe more cupboards," he says.

Felipe comes round to the end of the table where he can wave a finger at both of us. "You two are the only ones who know and you must forget that you do. For our family." We raise our glasses and swear to the contract. I try not to blurt out 'what'll you do with even more storage space'. We help them clear the table. We do the long goodbyes milling around in the kitchen. "I'm just going to use the loo. Bursting," I say.

I stumble upstairs and pee for hours in the main bathroom. I wash my hands and then I stop on the landing. The door of the nursery is ajar. In my mind I see Robert rushing in to the cry of a young child in the dark hours, with the world's only trans-dimensional time portal concealed above him until the next residents of this beautiful house remodel. The chance to explore the phenomenon, this cosmological enigma, will be lost, tucked away with the tide of childhood paraphernalia that will wash ever higher in the baby and the toddler years to come. The wind and the rain outside the house on St. John's Avenue have dropped. I move unsteadily but silently across the landing. I reach for the handle.

Stephen Narain

Stephen Narain was raised in Freeport, Bahamas by Guyanese parents, both educators who fled the Burnham dictatorship in 1982. A recipient of a John Thouron Prize for Study at Cambridge University, he earned an AB in English from Harvard College and an MFA in Fiction from the Iowa Writers' Workshop as a Paul and Daisy Soros New American Fellow. His work has appeared in Small Axe: A Platform for Caribbean Criticism, the Los Angeles Review of Books, Moko, and Wasafiri's special issue on the afterlives of indentured labor. In 2012, the NGC Bocas Lit Fest selected Stephen for its New Talent Showcase spotlighting promising Caribbean authors. Stephen lives in Orlando, where he is completing his first book, a coming-of-artist novel set between the West Indies and the United States in the 1950s and 1960s. He won the 2020 Bristol Short Story Prize.

WHAT IN ME IS DARK, ILLUMINE

Come, comrade stargazer.
Look at the sky I told you I had seen.
The glittering seeds that germinate in darkness.
And the planet in my hand's revolving wheel.
And the planet in my breast and in my head
and in my dream and in my furious blood.
Let me rise up wherever he may fall.
I am no soldier hunting in a jungle.
I am this poem like a sacrifice.

– Martin Carter, *Poems of Resistance
from British Guiana* (1954)

The Revolutionary doesn't look like a "Revolutionary." Doesn't possess Che Guevara's patchy beard, Fidel Castro's psycho eyes. Bredrin is shaped like a cricket player. Very slender, very strong. Bredrin speaks in Aristotelian paragraphs, his voice calm even at its crescendo. How does he manage this? This balance of sense and sensibility. This Walter Rodney. This "Brudda Wally." This Comrade Stargazer. Walter Rodney doesn't wear bell-bottoms. He wears an economics professor's Spring semester khakis, John-the-Baptist sandals, and a white shirt-jack stained beneath the armpits. His too-serious face is framed by horn-rimmed spectacles. His Afro is substantial enough to suggest an awareness of style's power, yet too tame to bleed into the territories of vanity. Style, his Afro suggests, is secondary to something else. But what? Anand is listening too hard; his listening is a performance. Tulsi can tell. This is love: knowing when your friend is putting on and breaking the mask. Quarter to nine. *Macbeth*, unfinished. Tulsi taps his toes. Bites his thumbnail. Begs Lord Ganesha to bring this meeting – and all its causes – to a swift, Aristotelian denouement.

They are assembled in Gobin's bottom house. Three weeks prior, a Working People's gathering in New Amsterdam had been raided by the Dictator's sycophants, a rebel arrested, accused of vandalizing a ministry office when six alibis – his wife, pregnant, included – swore the comrade was home tucking his son into bed.

"It getting late," Tulsi whispers in Anand's ear. "Let's go to Ling's."

Anand flashes him a look to let him know, despite Tulsi's scholarship, Anand still leads the pack. Their tastes change. Michel had put Tulsi onto Aerosmith, a band led by a white man with otherworldly sound, vulgar lips; Anand believes now in the logic of disco. Tulsi again reads the room: two dozen men, workers he has spent his whole life hellbent on not becoming. Men who work in the bauxite mines and on the sugar estates, men who wear sacks beneath their eyes, men who smell of salt and El Dorado rum which they nurse while the Revolutionary preaches.

"But Brudda Wally!" the big-skin man in the Booker polo shouts.

The man — Madeira and India in his veins — stands, rests a fat palm on his neighbor's shoulder.

"Steady-steady you ah go on about how we can mek it on we own, dat we can build tings fuh weself. But hear me good, nuh? We have dis jackass breathing over we. How we guh cause dem big-big change you ah preach about when we mouth always muzzle by de provisions we eating fuh live?"

The Revolutionary braces his backside against the purpleheart table. He takes a 750 milliliter bottle of 15-year and asks Comrade Beckles for his empty glass.

"Watch this glass," the Revolutionary says.

The Revolutionary pours the El Dorado into the glass until it flows onto the concrete ground.

Thou preparest a table before me in the presence of mine enemies: thou anointest my head with oil; my cup runneth over.

"Gosh, boy, Brudda Wally. Is wha really you ah try prove so?"

"Beckles, sometimes we brain so full up that we can't let new possibilities in."

"Alright, you make yuh point," Beckles says.

"How shall we empty our cups?" the Revolutionary asks.

Silently, Tulsi sucks his teeth. A sandfly feeds from his calf. He murders it.

Tulsi and Anand walk home. Anand wheels his motorbike between them.

"When a fella performs goodness so well – so consummately – what are his vices?"

"'Consummately?'" Anand repeats.

Kiskadees shriek. Involved in their own protest against insignificance.

The evening prior, Anand and Leela were lazing on Tulsi's verandah when Anand tossed a book onto Tulsi's lap.

How Europe Underdeveloped Africa

The cover: white hands tearing a red continent shaped like heartbreak.

"You know Brother Wally does write books?"

Anand asked the question like he were the Revolutionary's scribe. Anand, Lord Ganesha. The Revolutionary, Vyasa: a dictator. Tulsi observed how Leela handled the book. Like it were scripture. Tulsi disliked the cover. Something too Manichean about it. Who designed the cover? Had the artist known Europe – all its layers? Why do folks treat Africa like a country? A child?

"I hear Walter Rodney's a genius," Leela said. "Ph.D. at 24!"

Tulsi caresses the cover of *Macbeth*.

Donalbain: "There's daggers in men's smiles."

April 1977, Tulsi received an Alchemy Scholarship to study magical realism at the University of Toronto. For a Guyanese boy with middle class roots, there are many useless subjects you can study. But magical realism? How could Tulsi describe to this unbothered world the feeling of feeling a book inside oneself so wholly, so deeply, so unconditionally? Books ask you for nothing. Poetry makes nothing happen, could make anything happen – Auden. How could Tulsi describe the dignity and clarity he derived from reading, praying? The same dignity and clarity the Working People had been denied by Cain. Were you not meant to pursue the path that made you tremble and laugh and sweat when you step onto the bridge?

He and his friends finished watching "Saturday Night Fever" for the umpteenth time. Leela and her brother Bucket (so named because his head is shaped like a bucket). Fineman named Fineman because he is fat. Fatman named Fatman because he is not. Tulsi studies Anand. His best friend had gained twenty pounds, solid muscle. Spent the past year drinking milk, lifting weights. Anand looks like one of those dancers bred in Brooklyn from the film they just rewatched; Anand looks like a coolie John Travolta. Anand wears cream bell-bottoms and a too-tight shirt unbuttoned to his navel. He sports a hairstyle as close to an Afro an individual of Indian origin could possibly present to the summer street.

"Boy, it's why you showing off your body so?" Tulsi asks. "You looking like you have something to prove."

"Comrade, you know I making dis world better with alla dis sweetness."

"Call me anything, brother. But I ain't no 'comrade.'" Tulsi says.

Anand flinches, inches away. Tulsi wanted to hurt him – ever so slightly. Hurt him into a greater sense of focus. Responsibility. Reveal his pretenses. Break his mask.

"You coming to Ling's?" Anand asks. "What waiting for you home? Shakespeare? What Shakespeare have on Leela Persaud, eh?"

How he will miss her. This girl he wishes would fly back with him to Toronto, this girl who has no interest in leaving Georgetown or her family, no interest in snow or stone spires, a girl who is one with this place, who sings when she speaks, who dances as she walks, who works in her daddy's mechanic shop fixing cars, humming *The Tempest*.

"I should go back," Tulsi says.

"It's alright," Anand says. "I know you good. What you tink of dat book, eh?"

Tulsi has not yet read Walter Rodney's history. The street divides. Tulsi says goodbye to his friend – too abruptly, he knows, the question left fluttering in the night air like a monarch butterfly.

Tulsi does not want to ride on Anand's motorbike.

"Praise God you so maga," Anand says. "Hold tight. Leela and Bucket already reach."

Anand swooshes left, swerves right. Cars honk. Girls laugh. Anand flexes his bicep at the stop sign.

"Eh, boy, tek it easy," Tulsi says. "You driving too-too wild."

Anand kisses his teeth.

They fly into the wrong section of the city. Broken houses neighboring broken houses. Clothes hang between metal crosses on Calvary. Grey chickens dance and cluck. Tulsi searches for Pandit Brahma's temple on Cuffy Road. Searches for the scarlet jhandi flags. Inhales hard. Incense. Camphor. Clove.

Tulsi hops off the motorbike. Anand chains it to the gate. The puja has not yet begun. The courtyard buzzes, believers arranging the last of the oleanders onto iron plates. Women light votives. Fellows test tassa drums. Skinny fingers pluck sitar strings. Four girls, chamomile shalwars grazing the ground, carry Mother Durga on a bamboo dais. Mother's ten arms clutch weapons: arrows, a thunderbolt, a sword. Leela leads the procession. Tulsi imagines Leela in a wedding sari; he imagines placing a garland of white frangipani around her neck.

Tulsi's father never comes to puja despite all his insistence.

Son, Tulsi's father once told him, *plentyplenty fella siddung like saint whole day and chant dis and talk fatfat, but ask dem to give de shirt offa dem own back, eh? Suddenly pussyclat claw dem throat. Me forget if it was Jesus or Buddha or Bob Marley who say: "Show me yuh deeds. Show me yuh wuk." Hear me good, son. I don't worship no god. What I worship is Wuk.*

Dusk confuses the sky, an onslaught of gold. Old ladies bring out pholourie in straw baskets. Their daughters and granddaughters follow them with tamarind chutney, mango achaar. Pandit Brahma summons all the children to his feet, wraps a Chinese boy in his arms, the boy's eyes so intent he might as well had been glimpsing Mars. Or was it Jupiter? Tulsi leaves Anand with Bucket to stand by the fireside with Leela, frying mithai in sweet oil.

"Y'all ready fuh hear dis story bout Mother Durga?" Pandit Brahma asks.

Pandit Brahma tightens his bolo tie, slicks back his pompadour shiny with coconut oil. The children – two dozen lotuses – place index fingers on their lips, shush their neighbors, tug their earlobes.

"Long-long time ago," Pandit Brahma starts, "one demon – half-man, half-buffalo – want cause all kinda chaos pon dis world. No god nor goddess could kill he. Bredrin was scampish and skillfull, and dem two tings together, man, is a dangerous-dangerous pair. Dis demon mash up a whole heap of gods – like dis fella conscience evaporate in the sky. One day, Lord Vishnu, man – he couldn't take dis stchupidness no more, hear? He get mad-mad-mad. Mad-mad like when a man learn he own buddy wanna kill he. Dat kinda feeling. Like de sun betray he, like he ain't know if de earth gonna fall out from under he foot. One big-big beam of light start pouring outta Lord Vishnu mouth, and hear dis, nuh?! Light start pouring outta alla de mouths of every god de demon wound. From dis light, a goddess was born, and dis goddess name Mother Durga. Now, lemme give y'all de skinny pon de deal, eh? Mother Durga was no pushover. Wasn't bowing down to any scamp. Lady was a brick house. *BRICK HOUSE!* All dem gods, see? They donate they weapons – that's how come she ten hands get full up so. Now, when de demon sizing up Mother Durga, he getting real frighten, eh? I mean: he never see a woman cocky so. Mother Durga sitting pon top of a lion! Start galloping straight toward de demon, and de demon tink he could mash she up still, but he ain't measure de force of she will. Every time de demon shapeshift, Mother Durga adapt. You tink part of Mother Durga was frighten?" Pandit Brahma asks.

"NAHHHHH" the children scream.

"Can't be certain," Pandit Brahma says. "See, children, we wasn't there. Remember: be careful about what you say if you wasn't there. But safe to imagine Mother was cool. Calm. Collected. Just like Miss Diana Ross. De buffalo start charging, and Mother do something a lil bit different dis time. She stop. Stare straight into de demon eye. Study what evil look like. Record its shapes. Its colors. She breathe. Squint she two eye, open she third, reach for a simple, shiny trident, aim, steady – easy – like Lord Arjuna fighting a battle he ain't really wanna fight at all. Mother surrender, release. And do you think Mother made the final shot, my children?"

The children clap. Smile.

"Yes, my darlings. De demon's head was severed. But only cause Mother look at what no one dare look at before. I reckon Mother was a lil bit frighten. But she look. Still. And what she learn? Dat's above my pay scale, darlings. But if I have to guess, it might be something like dis: evil ain't 'evil' at all. Evil just grace waiting on the other side of fear."

Georgetown is Dutch and damp, the night sky sluggish, a prologue to the summer rain. Leela and he walk as one, Anand rolling his motorbike beside them. Palm trees black – asphalt even blacker than the pitch of its origin. The fat Queen Victoria is still missing her marble nose. A fellow quarrels with a rival in front of a tie-dye lorry. Mad Mr. Chin still fetches snacks atop his head – you have to give the fella marks for assiduousness – running up to Buicks and Bedfords when they stop at the light, exchanging toasted peanuts for coins with the grace of Double Nought Seven.

The Dictator banned wheat flour. Labeled dates and apples "imperialist." Tulsi worries for his mummy, her arms leaner, more sinewy – too muscular for a woman who worships sweets the way his daddy worships maths. She'd pound rice with a mortar and pestle just to make flour for roti.

You ah tell me, she sang. *Dat me nuh have nothing better fuh do with me time? Dat Burnham dotish, you hear me? You watch, one day me papers gonna come and boom: Mohini Ramkissoon gone! Y'all hear me?! Gone! I guh find my way to America by hook or by crook and cook so sweet, you bite yuh tongue.*

Tulsi is his mummy's son. Could care less for Guyana's politricks. Tulsi is committed to the food of art, to the art of food: to precision, to callaloo, to perfecting the subtlest of flavors. And this is the quality of the government Tulsi disdains the most: its clear lack of appreciation for the differences between a dahl made from channa and one made from split yellow peas.

"De truth," Anand says, turning the corner. "Is we dealing with de lesser of fifty evils, eh. Don't tink I naïve. You tink I believe everyting Brudda Wally say? Nah. God's eye: Pandit Brahma teach me dat. Fly above dis world, eh?! 10,000 miles. Look at what is what. Call a spade a spade. I know dis fella can't be Black Jesus. Besides, every messiah have he shame. But at least Brudda Wally – let's assume... true-true ting, dat's a dangerous habit: to assume – but let's assume dat alla dat history-learning, dat alla dat teaching, alla dat preaching, dat de way he look at he wife, dat de gentleness of he eyes, and alla dat genius – "

"He is a genius..." Tulsi says.

"Well, then, alla dat genius... let's assume we can trust if he gain power, he ain't guh forget he daddy was a tailor who give him de shirt he mend heself."

"He ain't guh survive," Leela says from nowhere.

And they both know exactly what she means. They walk her up to her door, wave to her parents.

"Who I cry fuh is he pickney," Leela says. "When dat demon murder dat professor, what Brudda Wally wife s'posed to say to she child?"

To progress, Pandit Brahma taught. *You can't trust lazily, can't always siddung and expect some savior to run to yuh side. Sometimes, a demon might rub up next to you; sometimes, dat demon might be yuh own kin. Nah, boy. Sometimes, you have to flip. You ain't know Mother Kali? You ain't know how she does run off? Man, when she start, you ain't wanna be fifty miles too-too close to she madness: mother chop of yuh head if you block de path to she goal.*

Tulsi sits on the verandah with his family, his mummy nibbling apostatic dates. Mohini Ramkissoon uses that carnival of misery, that festival of guns to her advantage: to take laughter more seriously. Her philosophy? *Man, if Burnham guh kill you, might as well speak all dem words dat deh pon yuh mind.* His daddy's belly is full: sweet gilbaka curry, potato roti, three types of dahl. Tulsi told them he ate at the puja. All he wanted was tea – extra cream.

Tulsi knows they are proud of him. You just know these things – can't pretend. They don't mind he is studying madmen: Márquez and Borges. Carpentier. They don't understand their only child, but they love what they don't understand, and he loves them for loving what they don't understand, and this is love: allowing your child back into the circle even when he risks metamorphosing into the Prodigal Son.

Tulsi loves his friends in Toronto even though they do not fully understand the texture, the music of Guyana. (Does he?) Part of them believes he lives in some complicated paradise, and he allows them to speak so he could learn what they think. He refused every spliff he was offered.

"I mean, my man, you're telling me you don't smoke the ganja every day?" Michel asked.

Michel was a genial bear. That first time Tulsi met Michel's girlfriend, Clementine, he wondered what the Caribbean sun would do to her skin.

"Where are you from?" she asked him in her rhythm: raspy, Québécois.

"Guyana," he said and felt peculiar pronouncing the country like a mantra.

"Ghana?" Clementine asked.

"No. Guyana," Tulsi repeated. "Ghana, West Africa. Guyana: South America."

Clementine searched Michel's room for an atlas.

"West of Suriname," Tulsi said only to realize that explanation likely did not help her confusion. "Brazil," Tulsi decided. "North of Brazil."

"But it's like Jamaica, no?!" Michel asked, inhaling his doobie, exhaling an O in the air. "I mean: you talk like the Bob Marley."

Michel has the tendency to place a definite article in front of the names of men he believes are destined for Zion. Tulsi surrendered. Nearing five deadlines, his bedsheets were wet with quiet cortisol.

"Yes," he said. "Imagine Jamaica. In South America."

"Like how Quebec is a French country in Canada," Michel explained.

"Oui," Tulsi said, lifting Blue Mountain coffee to his lips.

Tulsi sets down his cup of tea.

"Daddy," he says.

"Yes, comrade."

Tulsi elbows his father – God, how Tulsi will miss him.

"I have a question… dis Brother Wally?" Tulsi asks. "Wha you tink of he?"

"Me nuh know, boy. You know yuh father – mind he own business. I try nuh fuh get mix up in dem sorta tings."

"Seem bright," his mummy says. "Good looking. Beautiful family."

"Anand invite me to a rally. Friday," Tulsi says. "You tink I should go?"

"Might do you some good," his daddy says. "'Certainly, when Judgment Day comes, we shall not be asked what books we have read, but what deeds we have done – '"

"'We shall not,'" Tulsi continues. "'Be asked how well we have debated, but how devoutly we have lived.'"

His mummy shakes her head, cracks her knuckles – that sly half-smile.

"You wanna go?" she asks Tulsi.

No, his Third Eye tells him.

"No," he says. "But Anand might be cross."

"Sweetheart," his mummy says. "So smart and so slow. Darling, ain't you know? Anand done figure he best friend done buy a one-way ticket to Mars."

Anand grips his satchel.

"Stay with yuh girl," Anand says. "You ain't remember what Brother Marcus say? 'You can leave life right now – let that determine what you say and do and think.'"

Tulsi smiles a sly half-smile. When Tulsi went to return Walter Rodney's book to Anand, Tulsi gave Anand a slim volume of the

Meditations of Marcus Aurelius.

"Take Walter Rodney back to Toronto. Re-read him," Anand said. "Man, dat Emperor Marcus: like he proper get burn by life."

"I teaching you to dance. Tonight!" Leela says. "I mean you a shame, man. To yuh country. To de Caribbean. Come home. Tonight."

"But Uncle Roger?" Tulsi says.

"Daddy respect you – you know dat. Real bad. Call you a gentleman."

Anand waves. Tulsi and Leela observe him walk to the rally. A part of Tulsi walks with Anand. Tulsi doesn't want to look at Leela, not just then, and she knows why.

"Just come, boy. I get dat Bee Gees vinyl! Groovy ting! We lime on de verandah. Tonight, I don't think it supposed to rain."

Leela's dance lessons don't last too-too long.

"How a man can live in Guyana he whole life and move like a chicken getting ready fuh dead, eh?"

"I dat bad?"

"Boy, whatever you doing beyond apology. Stop. Let we sit down."

Leela pulls Tulsi by the thumb, leads him to the hammock on her verandah. Lights the kerosene lamp. Rubs lemon and eucalyptus on his arms to repel the sandflies. With the Bee Gees silent, that night could sing.

"You know dat Third Eye Pandit Brahma steady going on about?" Leela asks. "When you open it, you know what I realize? You can't think so much. Darling, dat's why you can't dance as good as I know you can. You always thinking so-so much. Holding your cards so close to dat chest; you never permit yourself to just play. Your pride is your brain – that's de mark of you (you think). But, darling, I like you fuh more than your brain."

"For what?"

"For one, man, I don't know."

Leela pauses.

"I like looking at you," she says.

Tulsi had long reasoned his corporeality is some limited vessel designed to trap quantum light.

"'O, dah dis too-too solid flesh wuh melt,'" Tulsi says, setting his hand on Leela's thigh.

Leela looks behind her, doesn't flinch.

"Hamlet: dat madass," Leela says. "First soliloquy. Don't tink I wasn't listening dat day."

"I know you was listening. Dat's why I want you come with me. One day."

Tulsi moves his hand to her shoulder, dreaming of what it would be like: for he and Leela to become man and wife.

"Where?" Leela asks. "To Canada? Like you fall on you head, eh. Just cause I know my Shakespeare don't mean I have to leave my Guyana."

"Dat's not what I mean," Tulsi says.

"Then what you mean?" Leela asks. "I ain't gonna say de brutal ting, man, like I think you think you too good fuh we."

"You just said it."

"But I brighter than that, comrade. Fact is you here with me and dese sandflies on dis same verandah. And you here with Anand. And you love us, and we love you, and, sorry, but dah nuh guh change."

"I coming back."

Leela's kiss-teeth is a zealot's scream.

"God say don't lie. You ain't coming back, boy. You gonna stay. Or fly to Inglan. Darling, you guh flyyy... I know you. Where you steady running on about? Dat Cambridge. Dat Cambridge gonna catch you. You know dat's de school Viola Chambers go?"

Tulsi imagines Leela reading at Cambridge.

"And you wouldn't come?" he asks.

Leela sighs, looks to her feet, to Tulsi – to the stars.

"My Tulsi," Leela says, brushing nothing from his eyebrows. "Same Tulsi. So smart and so slow. Darling, Mother Durga ain't teach you? You try walk left and right de same time – you gonna end up de selfsame spot."

Valerie O'Riordan

Valerie O'Riordan is Senior Lecturer in English Studies at the University of Bolton, where she is Programme Leader for English and Creative Writing. Her short fiction has been published widely and she won the Bristol Short Story Prize in 2010 and the O. Henry Prize in 2019.

MUM'S THE WORD

Three times with his grunting and the calloused hand over my mouth: first, the kitchen wall rough at my back; second, hands and knees against the splintered attic floor; third, pushing me into the thin mattress, while my mother slept in the next room, her belly swollen and taut. Then a sticky wrap of silver paper, chocolate to slip into my pocket on the way to school. Hands and legs all sticky, and neither of us speaking.

When the time came, they rammed a tongs between my mother's legs, but all they got out was a tangled grey-face thing that took a single half-hearted breath. My mother was split open. I heard her screaming. Later I helped my aunts boil the bedsheets: we scoured and bleached them, but finally they sent me out to dump them in the skip in the back alley. I bundled the rest up too, the stained knickers and the ripped tights, wrapped them up in the pillowcase where nobody would see. I crouched in the dark beside the metal bin and vomited, a watery spew all over my good shoes. He was watching me from the kitchen window when I came back up the path, my hand on my stomach. He said, it's the two of us now, girl, and held me by the shoulder. His face was red and wet.

When I couldn't go to school anymore, the clothes straining to cover me, my armpits stained with the sweat of my bulk, he left me alone. My shadow on the bedroom wall in the moonlight was like the moon itself, round and still. I heard him coming in when the light was trickling over the treetops, his steps back and forth in the corridor, his sobbing through the wall. My aunts had stopped visiting when he stopped letting them inside; I sweated and pushed on my own, and the baby screamed. He had it brought away; the social worker shook her head as she swaddled it and said love, a big girl like you, didn't you take precautions? His arm around my shoulder, fingers kneading, as he said, I'll keep a better eye on her, Miss, don't you worry.

Diana Powell

Diana Powell's stories have featured in a number of competitions, such as the 2019 Chipping Norton Literature Festival Prize (winner), the 2020 Society of Authors ALCS Tom-Gallon Trust Award (runner-up) and the 2020 TSS Cambridge Prize (3rd place). Her work has appeared in several anthologies and journals, including 'Best (British) Short Stories 2020' (Salt), and in her collection 'Trouble Crossing the Bridge' (available on Kindle). She has also published a novella, *Esther Bligh* (Holland House. 2018) and a novel, *things found on the mountain*, which was published by Seren Books in 2023. She won the 2022 Cinnamon Press Literature Award with her novella, *The Sisters of Cynvael*, which is due out in 2024. She was the winner of the 2023 Bristol Short Story Prize. She has a website www.dianapowellwriter.com and can be found on FaceBook and Twitter (@diana_p_writer).

A CURE FOR ALL OUR ILLS

They are taking us to the church again.

Our mothers, sisters, maids, leading us up the breathless holloways or along the ancient drove paths.

It is the same when they bring the animals, except *those* are tethered, nose or neck, with brass rings and leather halters. They don't do that to us. Not yet. No more than the grip of bony fingers beneath the elbow, a pinch, the press of ragged nails into our tender flesh, to guide us, now and then.

Today, there are two others approaching the crossroads.

That means there will be three of us today. There have been more in the past. Six, I remember, once. When a girl no longer appears, I like to think it is because she has 'improved'. There is no need for her to come any more. But it is not always so.

At the crossroads, we come together, shuffle our feet, bow our heads, then peek up through our hair. Perhaps we recognise each other from before, unless there is a new girl – as I was once, as we all were.

Most of us come from the farms. This is a farming county, in a farming country, after all. Wales. Perhaps there will be a cluster of houses. Or an occasional cottage. There are a few Big Houses – a rectory, a manor. But mostly farms.

Esther, who keeps her head lowest, is from a farm up and down the hill. The other, Lizzie, who was new last time, doesn't quite know where she comes from. And there is me, Sarah. I am one of those from a Big House. The one you might see, if you climbed to the top of the church tower, and looked west from there, towards the ocean. But they do not allow us to climb up the tower, nor any high place.

Sometimes we say hello. Sometimes we don't. Those who lead us may exchange a few words about the weather. The weather is important in a farming community.

We move on to the church together.

The church always looks lonely. It stands there, on its own, the nearest dwelling hidden behind the trees. It belongs to a saint no-one knows anything about, or why he should have a church here. Nothing like his/our Patron, with his Cathedral resting in the nearby vale, dedicated there, and in every parish. *This* saint went elsewhere quickly, it is said. Perhaps he was as lonely as his church.

It has a tall, thin tower, thinner than most. It is of dark stone, with gaps etched for windows. No bright patchwork glass here. No wash of slaking lime to cheer it.

Everything about it is dour.

We are not here for the church.

That is what people mistake.

Thinking we have come to have the Lord bless us, his saint bless us (whoever that saint is), thinking we have come here to pray for His Son's Saving. Because Jesus can do that.

No.

It is nothing like that.

We are led around the building, into the churchyard that circles around the church. A circular bound means something, the Wise Folk, the grandmothers and Dyn Hysbys say. It has something to do with beliefs far older than God, Christ, their saints, known or unknown. *That* is why we are here.

'Eat,' they say – our mothers, sisters, maids, whoever has brought us.

'Eat!'

The cattle have been here before us, we can see. No more than a few hours ago, the deep imprints of their hooves, churning the ground to mud, so there is meagre grass left. Among the mud, their ordure is mixed in. Their urine fills the clefts in the ground.

Esther begins to cry.

'Come on now, eat.' They wander away then. Perhaps they wish to talk more about the weather.

'Look, there,' I say, spying a patch beneath the hedge ignored or unnoticed by the cattle. 'Perhaps there...'

I am allowed to bring a blanket – I am from the Big House, after all. I spread it out, near the untouched spot, and the three of us sit down.

Anyone passing might think we are here for a picnic.

Three young ladies on an outing. Yes, they have chosen a rather strange spot, but, still…

Three young ladies making most of their leisure by eating out of doors.

And yes, they are about to eat something. Look!

But no, we are not here for a picnic.

I pluck a handful of the grass, wipe it on the leaves in the hedge, then give some to each of the girls.

Lizzie takes a blade between her thumb and forefinger, and touches it to her teeth. It is, after all, only her second visit. Her face is lost in gurns and ruffles.

Esther and I chew solidly, our eyes fixed on some distant place. We have found it the best way.

In the beginning, in the time the Wise Folk talk about, there was no need to eat the grass. A spring came out of the ground, in the middle of the circle. That was when they noticed it, they say. Perhaps it was just one cow first – a favourite milker drying up, attacking the hand that fed it. Or a dog. Perhaps it was a dog. A gentle beast, who started growling at its shadow and barking at the clock in the hall. And then… droplets of spit, seething at the mouth, so they knew, for sure. The Sickness. And perhaps this cow, or that dog, wandered into this field by chance, his master in pursuit, and stopped to drink at the spring, as if drawn to it, having refused all other water.

Perhaps the foaming stopped then, together with the strange behaviour, and the creature was cured. They tell.

And all other suffering animals were brought from round about, and they were cured, too.

So then the people were brought.

Perhaps.

Lizzie shucks the shred of grass from her lips, pulls a doll from the pocket of her apron. She holds it tight, and rocks it from side to side. They gave it to her when they took her baby from her, she told us, last time. The baby she wasn't supposed to have. 'You are too young to have babies,' her mother said. 'You are unwed,' her father shouted. The baby wasn't supposed to happen, yet it did. And then it wasn't there. She croons to the doll, instead.

I tell Lizzie about the spring, thinking to help her understand why she is here.

'But I do not have the Sickness,' she says.

Lizzie is right. True, bubbles of spit formed at her lips, as they took her baby away. And she screamed and tore at the flesh of those nearest her. And true, since then, she has spent most of her days sitting in the corner, rocking her doll. But no, she does not have the Sickness.

'After a while,' I continue, 'they built the church, and the well dried up. The Sickness returned, until another poor, stricken animal strayed into the churchyard, ate the grass and was cured. 'The power of the spring has found its way into the grass,' they proclaimed. The church claimed it most, requiring all those who ate the grass to make some payment for the honour. Hence, the hole in the wall for our pennies. 'A small price to pay to rid you of the Sickness!' they said.'

'But I do not have the Sickness, either,' says Esther.

Esther sees things. Strange beings floating in front of her. Or places where she would like to go – green meadows, a lake – until they disappear.

When this happens, she shakes, cannot talk, and does not want to eat. She cannot sleep.

All this is just before her Bleeding, until after it.

They have had a doctor to examine her beneath. Then another, looking deeper into her, prodding and poking. They have tried this potion and that liniment, '*down there*'. There is talk of Esther being sent away. Of being locked up. They lock her up, now. Those days before, during and after her Bleeding.

In between, they send her to eat the grass.

'Later, it is said they put the grass between slices of bread and butter. Thick slices of farmhouse bread, spread with rich yellow butter, straight from the dairy. And fresh, lush grass, washed and patted dry, laid neatly, so that it sunk into the golden cream, lost there. There was a name for it, even. A Welsh name, being in Wales. *Porfar cynddeiriog*. As if it were special.'

Yes, indeed, in those days, it would most certainly appear that we were on a picnic, with our neatly cut sandwiches spread on our blanket, ready to eat.

'But they grew tired of this over time. Or forgot it. Just as they forgot the grass was for the Sickness – forgot, even, the Sickness, except for the farmers, wanting succour for their cows. 'Why not try it for other ailments?' someone said. 'These strange ailments suffered by young women, that there are no cures for. Why not just bring them here, and tell them to eat?' So they did.'

It was my governess who told me all this. I come from the Big House, after all. Rich enough to have a governess to teach me my lessons. Miss Marchant. Catherine. She told me all this as she was packing her bags; she, trying to explain to me, as I explain to Lizzie.

Grass meant something other, before Cat left. Grass was for lying in, beside her, after we had swum in the lake. We laughed at our naked bodies streaked green. She licked my stained skin, then we swam again. The water washed over us. 'We are pure,' we thought.

'Dirty, filthy. The sin of the Devil. Unholy.' – these were the words they used for her.

I, the child, was ill or sick. They brought me here, straight away. 'Eat,' they said.

'Neither do I have the Sickness,' I say.

Esther is beginning to retch.

This is something that happens. It is what happens with dogs, after all – they, choosing to eat the grass when they need to rid something noxious from their innards. Is this what our guardians think? That we will retch up our ailments? Or our sins? That they are sins? That the demons, devils – whatever is inside our hearts, minds, stomachs – will rise up through our mouths?

They – those who have brought us today – have wandered out of sight, searching for somewhere to chew cud of their own, it might be said.

'Come,' I say, to Esther and Lizzie. We get up. I take their hands. 'Let us go into the church, and climb up the tower. It would be nice to see the world from there.'

And yes, it is nice, when we reach the top, and look out across the land, the wind blowing through our hair.

And yes, as I thought, if we look past the fields, across to the dell where the Patron Saint's cathedral is cradled, we can see a circle of blue, caught between the trees. The lake. A bird's flight away.

Below, those who brought us – our mothers, sister, maids – have realised our absence, and come to look for us, and spotted us up here.

They are waving to us, shouting. 'Come down,' they say.

We wave back.

'What shall we do?' I ask Esther and Lizzie. 'Shall we go back down, or wander further?'

'Down' is the muddy grass where the cattle trample, sending the gravestones upwards, at strange angles. Coffins have been pushed to the surface in wet winters, the wind has splintered the wood, the corpses within seeping into the earth. And there is the venting of the beasts. And there is so little grass left now, besides. What kind of cure could it give?

Ahead, is the emerald green sward, with the lake beyond. Blue sky, green, green, grass, lapping water, all so beautiful and pure.

Which shall we choose?

We take each other's hands, and step forward.

***

We are going to the church again, today.

We walk arm in arm, up the holloway and along the drove path, chatting, laughing, the three of us. Esther, Lizzie and me.

At the crossroads, we meet Lucy, Mari, Mary and Bet – the girls I remember from before. We greet each other, then go on, waving at another group, who are wending across the fields.

Yes, a dozen young ladies in all. Anyone seeing us might think we are out for a ramble in the countryside, or a 'rendezvous' for conversation and merriment. A 'divertissement' such as young ladies enjoy!

But no, that is not why we are here.

We move into the circle of the churchyard together.

Now, we must stop our chatter, and turn our upward mouths down, gritting our faces into pictures of sadness, while we gather around the open grave, waiting for its coming incumbent.

That is why we are here.

The Sickness returned in the summer, the worst it had ever been, afflicting our mothers, sisters, maids; our fathers, brothers, labourers, taking so many from us, from our small farming community. *This* burial is the latest of many, with the graves butting against each other, filling every last corner of the cemetery, pushing up more of the grass than any of the beasts' hoof-prints, destroying any left-over growth more fully than the ordure and urine, the rotting corpses, the winter weather.

Only the few farmers who recalled the words of the Wise Folk stay well. And us. The girls who had been made to eat the grass, as a cure for all our unfathomable ills. We, too, remain unscathed.

So we come to mourn each death, being the only ones fit and able to do so, and pray to the saint (whoever he may be) and his Patron, and our Lord and His Son; pray that the dead's souls go to the place they deserve (wherever that place may be). And thank Them, too, quietly, under our breath, for what we have received.

Stefanie Seddon

Stefanie Seddon grew up on a farm in New Zealand. After moving to the UK, she worked in the City of London before completing an MA in Creative Writing at Birkbeck, University of London. Stefanie's short stories have won the Bristol Short Story Prize and the Commonwealth Short Story Prize for Europe and Canada, and been shortlisted for the Pindrop Royal Academy Short Story Prize. Her short fiction has been published online by Granta, Adda and TSS Publishing, and has appeared in The Bristol Short Story Prize Anthology Volume 9, The Mechanics Institute Review and Schweitzer Monat. Her non-fiction work has been published online at *The Independent*.

KĀKAHU

There are lots of ways to remember that day; the day I became a bird. Salt and pine needles, breathed through treetops. A red-gold light on folded wings. I remember other things, too. Like, it was the last day of the school term. And it was the first time I'd heard my mum get up before me. I'd listened to her sounds; slippers scuffing, a Panadol fizzing in a glass, the flick of a lighter. We sat at the table, the two of us. Me in school uniform with a bowl of cornflakes. Her in pyjamas opposite; a lit Bensons dangling from bone-white fingers, smoke rising into stringy blond hair. Mum's eyes brightened when I told her about the prize-giving ceremony that evening. You'll have to tell me all about it, she said. When the cigarette burnt down to her fingertips, I'd pushed an ashtray under her hand.

She'd had a letter from school about Tama.

"He hasn't been in all week," she said, scratching at her arms.

Tama hadn't been home all week, either. The Sunday before, some people had turned up. These were people Mum used to know in Auckland; people she'd come to Toroa Bay to get away from. She'd paced up and down behind the curtain like a fly tripping though a cobweb. Then she'd opened the door and welcomed them in. Tama took me off to the beach all day, but when we got back they were still there, sitting around the table like ghosts, foil strewn everywhere. I'd recognised that look on Mum's face. It was like she wasn't really there. Tama went mad. He called her all sorts of names on his way out and when he got to the gate, he kicked the rubbish bin so hard it toppled over.

I glanced at the letter, lying in folds by the ashtray.

"Tama's sixteen, Mum," I said. "He can leave school whenever he wants."

I rinsed my bowl and opened the curtains.

"You're a good girl, Marama," said Mum, fixing her eyes on the wall.

"I've gotta go, Mum," I said.

Outside, the sun was rising over the macrocarpa hedge, drying the rotting timbers at the corners of our house. Mrs Sullivan waved as I crossed the road. I was the only person in my family who spoke to the neighbours, what with Mum staying indoors and Tama not being the type you'd want to complain to about the noise. He'd shaved all his hair off in the winter and started getting tattoos up his arms. Sometimes I just didn't recognise my big brother, even though he looked exactly like me.

"Morning Mrs Sullivan," I said.

Mrs Sullivan was a tall, thin lady with an owlish face and gnomes in her flower beds. The spray from her hose made a rainbow across the grass. It was hard to walk past without stopping.

"Hello, Marama," she said. "You look very smart."

"It's the prize-giving tonight. We have to wear our ties."

"Are you enjoying the books, dear?"

"I am," I said. "Thank you."

A few weeks after we'd moved in, Mrs Sullivan had come over with a cardboard box full of old books and magazines. She was going to take them to the charity shop, she'd said, but she'd seen me sitting on the steps and thought I might like a rummage. Halfway down, I'd found a book called *The Encyclopaedia of Maori Myths*. Tama had seen me reading it and hooted. Someone's finally written a book about Dad, he said. That had kicked it all off with Mum, and I'd ended up taking the book across the road to the pine forest and reading it up a tree.

Past Mrs Sullivan's was a row of faded wooden bungalows; sweetshop squares of pastel pinks and lemons. On the other side of the street, the pine plantation separated the village from a bank of rolling sand dunes that bordered the beach.

The bus stop was at the corner. I sat on a wall and swung my bare legs against the concrete. The waves came as a whisper; surf crashing on silver sand, blown across the dunes, filtered through conifer branches. The air was spiced with sea kelp and cut wood; the sea and the forest all mixed together. When we'd first moved out here, we'd walked along this track to the highest part of the sand dunes, where you could see the wide, flat coastline curving all the way back to Auckland. Tama and me took running jumps off the steepest banks, tumbling, out of control through clumps of golden marram grass. Mum lay back on the fine, warm sand and when I'd scrambled up to lie beside her, it had felt like we were a very long way from the city. It smells like a new start, Marama, she said.

When I looked up, the bus was rumbling towards my stop. I slung my schoolbag over my shoulder and climbed on board.

"Tēnā koutou tamariki! Good morning Year Five!"

Mrs Parata swept into the classroom, a tornado of patterned violet tearing through school-grey cotton. Mrs Parata's shoulders measured as wide as her bosom, her bosom as wide as her hips. She stood in front of the class, blocking out the whiteboard.

"E noho, Jayden. And you too, Manu, sit down! In your seats everyone, please."

Mrs Parata's short black hair had fine white streaks and sprouted up from her forehead like Queen Elizabeth's. It never moved, even when she drove up to the school in her little red convertible. If I had a granny, I'd thought, I'd want her to look like Mrs Parata.

We had her for an hour, three mornings a week. Her Year Five Te Reo Māori classes had begun badly, last February. Returning to school after a long, hot summer, we'd fidgeted and sighed over thick text books as sunlight breached the narrow classroom window. In March, Mrs Parata changed tactic. She'd started telling us stories. Tales of mischievous fairies, lovers pushed apart by a forest god, beautiful maidens carried off by fierce taniwha. She brought us things to look at; she called them taonga – treasures. She showed us an old spear, black and white photographs of tattooed Maori women in crinkled Victorian dresses, a handful of red soil.

Once, she made us write down a memory on a piece of paper and we took it in turns to read them aloud. Memories are taonga too, she said. Most kids had talked about old people who'd died. Their great grandparents, or special aunties and uncles. Kavesi had spoken about going back to see his cousins in Samoa. When it was my turn, I told them about the time Mum gave Tama and me ten bucks each and we'd hitchhiked to the shopping mall. We'd bought some chips and spent the rest in the arcade and when Tama won a helium dolphin balloon on the rifle range, he'd tied the string around my wrist. I walked back to my seat to sniggers and whispers and then Mrs Parata asked me some stuff in Māori about the dolphin; what colour it was and how long it stayed up in the air – things like that.

"Today," said Mrs Parata, "I have something *very* special to show you. Can I have some help please boys?"

She beckoned Alastair and Ricky to the corridor. Seconds later, they shuffled backwards into the classroom carrying between them a headless shop mannequin, draped in a bulky cover. It rustled as they moved.

"Gently... gently now," said Mrs Parata. "A little nearer the window. That's it. Right there, in the light."

She hurried to the window and pushed it open. Then she marched to the front of the classroom and laid her hand on the mannequin's shoulder.

"He aha tēnei? Does anyone know what this might be?"

"A suit of armour," said Yi-Chang.

"A dead body," said William.

"Let's find out," said Mrs Parata, scanning the room. "Who would like to unzip the front? Marama?" I shrank into my chair, picking at the staples in my exercise book.

"No? All right, Yi-Chang. Haere mai. Come up the front please."

Yi-Chang, a cheerful Taiwanese boy with close-cropped hair and braces, bounded up to the mannequin and grasped the zip. It caught halfway down and Mrs Parata grabbed his hands to stop him tugging. Gently, she unsnagged the metal pull and together they lowered it to the bottom. A blaze of copper burst out from the cover and Yi-Chang stepped back quickly.

It was a cloak, the colour of flames, entirely covered in feathers. The room stirred; breath sucked in sharply; soft whistling. Some kids pushed out their chairs and stood, leaning over their desks, open-mouthed. I don't remember exactly what I was doing. I just know I couldn't take my eyes off that cloak. Caught in the light, it rippled in sunburnt-orange and tangerine-red; it had streaks of gold, amber and bronze, speckles of eggshell brown.

Mrs Parata was the first to speak.

"This is a *Kākahu*, a cloak. It's special, because it's been woven with feathers from the kaka bird, a very big parrot."

I had seen Māori cloaks before, mainly on TV. Old people on the news, sitting around while politicians made speeches. But none of those cloaks were as beautiful as this.

After a long time, Grace put up her hand.

"Where's it from?"

"It came to me from my Aunty," said Mrs Parata. "And before that, it came from her Nannie Kora, who was a weaver. I believe it was Nannie Kora who made it."

"What's it for?" said Yi-Chang, still standing at the front. "What do you *do* with it?"

"I'll wear it tonight, Yi-Chang. A cloak made from red or orange feathers should be worn for a special occasion, like tonight's prize-giving. This will be my academic cloak."

I pictured the teachers, stern and serious in their flowing black gowns, looking down at their pupils like crows on a rooftop. Then I imagined Mrs Parata, striding across the stage in a blaze of scarlet, wrapped in this treasure from her Aunty's grandmother.

Mrs Parata was chuckling.

"I'll tell you something my mokopuna say to me. They say: 'Hey, Nannie, he kūkū ki te kāinga, he kākā ki te haere.'" Mrs Parata pronounced the words slowly, holding her hands up as if she was conducting an orchestra. "It means 'a pigeon at home, a parrot abroad.' I guess that's what I'll be tonight."

"Did the birds die?" said William.

Mrs Parata nodded gravely. "A lot of birds," she said. "At least sixty or seventy."

William stretched an arm out in front and squeezed a finger around an invisible trigger. He made the sound of a machine gun.

Mrs Parata lifted some feathers at the front of the cloak.

"That brightest orange you see, there," she said. "It comes from the kaka's underwing."

"I reckon you'll look like a bird!" said Kevisi, laughing.

"Yes," said Mrs Parata. "I suppose I will."

"Big Bird," muttered Alastair.

Holly put up her hand. "What's that speckled patch at the front, Mrs Parata?"

"Good question Holly. Come closer, class, and have a look at this tuft."

The class surged forward. Sprouting between Mrs Parata's pressed fingers was a clump of light brown feathers, about the size of a chocolate biscuit, patterned with black lines and speckles, clearly distinct from its bed of crimson red.

"Does anyone know what this might be?" she said.

"Gravy," said Ricky. "Your aunty was a messy eater, eh."

"Ha ha," said Alastair. "Ha ha ha."

"Put your hand up when you want to speak," said Mrs Parata. She pointed at a mousy, freckled girl with large glasses. "Yes, Emma?"

"They're put there by the weaver," said Emma. "They're signature feathers."

"Well done," said Mrs Parata. "Signature feathers. This is the weaver signing her name to her work. Sending a message about herself."

"A message to who?" said Kevisi.

"To the wearer, usually," said Mrs Parata. "But who else might the weaver be communicating with?" The classroom was silent.

Seventy birds, I thought. I pictured it around my shoulders, heavy and rustling. I felt bold. I stepped back from the group and put up my hand.

"With me," I called.

Alastair snorted. Heat rushed up to my face. A hard lump went the other way, down my neck and into my guts. I stared at my sandals.

"Marama's right," said Mrs Parata. "Did everyone hear that? Say that again, Marama, and speak up this time."

I could barely hear Mrs Parata above the thump in my ears. But I was in it now. I took a deep breath.

"She's communicating... with... me?" I said, fading to a whisper.

"You are *so* weird," said Ricky, sideways.

Mrs Parata raised her voice.

"Marama has just pointed out that this could be a message to all of us. The weaver is *speaking* to the onlooker, sending a message through her signature feathers. The patterns show us what she was thinking about at the time."

"What?" said Grace, wide-eyed. "What was she thinking?"

"Well," said Mrs Parata, slowly. "She has used some rare feathers here – kiwi – so she might have been telling us something about her mana, her stature. Or, possibly, about the mana of the wearer."

"Kiwi!" said Grace. "You can't kill a kiwi."

"Not now," said Mrs Parata. "But this is a very old cloak."

As the class gathered round the cloak, I slunk back to my seat. I leaned my head on the desk and thought about the birds in the cloak. My red book said that birds were the children of Tāne-mahuta – strong, courageous Tāne, god of the forest. It was Tāne who covered his Mother Earth in tall trees and ferns and it was Tāne who let birds fly. It said that some birds were messengers; that they helped people to communicate with the spirit world. I was staring out the window when the lunch bell went and the classroom emptied around me.

"Marama?" said Mrs Parata. "Are you alright?"

She was hoisting the cover back onto the cloak.

"Yes," I said, my face feeling hot again.

She pulled up the zip and walked the mannequin across the floor to the corner.

"I'll see you tonight, then," she said.

"OK."

She stopped at the door, holding the handle.

"You can look at the cloak again, if you'd like."

"OK," I said. "Thank you."

I liked being alone in the classroom. If you sat on your own in the playground, you could bet a teacher would come along and ask you what the problem was. I tapped my fingers on the desk and took a bag of crisps and a Pepsi out of my bag. The window was still open and I noticed that the light was really streaming in now, bathing the front row in a yellow haze. I moved up to Yi-Chang's seat to finish my lunch and I guess that's when I got the idea to move the mannequin out of its dark corner. I dragged it around the front of Mrs Parata's desk, setting it upright directly in the path of the sun. Then I unzipped the cover and slipped it off.

I pressed my hands on the feathers. They were smooth and light, like strips of ribbon. I laid my cheek in the down and it smelled of old wood. I put my arms around it, hugging it so tightly my arms ached. Sometime after that, I slipped it off the mannequin and wrapped it around my shoulders. I had the wings of a bird; 'the wing-flapping children of Tāne', that's what it called us in my book. I swirled around and the cloak's black and white edging swept the floor like a broom. I imagined myself at the prize-giving, singing the karanga to welcome the parents. I was Mrs Parata. I was a bird.

Then I heard a clatter of plastic and a loud, long fizz. Brown liquid trickled over the front of Yi-Chang's desk. An empty Pepsi bottle bounced off the floor. I looked down at the cloak. A dark stain seeped into the signature feathers; the light, delicate kiwi feathers put there by Nannie Kora.

It was panic, I guess, that made me do it.

I threw the cloak off my shoulders, rolled it up on the floor like a sleeping bag, and stuffed it deep into my school bag. I heard some tiny snaps, like bones, breaking, but there was just no way I could get it to fit in. Then I saw Manu's cricket bag wedged between the legs of his chair. His bag was deep and long and had straps that could go over your shoulders. I tipped Manu's bat and gloves and padding into a pile under his desk and placed the rolled-up cloak inside. Then I zipped up the bag and I ran. I ran out of the classroom, out of the school grounds and all the way to the bottom of Ferguson Avenue until I reached the second bus stop past the school.

I had to wait twenty minutes at that bus stop. Across the street, a yellow flowering kowhai tree waved over someone's garden. Plain, brown birds tripped along its branches. On the bus home, I thought things through. I'd go home and sponge out the brown marks from Mrs Parata's cloak. Then I'd take it carefully back to school, put it on the mannequin, and Mrs Parata would find everything back to normal by prize-giving.

It was half past one when the bus pulled in to Toroa Bay. My house looked still and quiet like it always did when Tama was out. When I got to the door, I fumbled around for the key in my school bag. I put the key in the lock. I opened the door. I looked for Mum.

She was there, lying on the sofa, with her eyes open. The curtains had been closed so I pulled them back and the room filled with light. I went right up close to Mum and that's when I saw that I was wrong. She was cold. She wasn't there at all.

Pine trees are the best for climbing. Their branches are sturdy and perfectly spread for a strong foothold on the way up; for gripping tightly on the way down. The trunk takes you straight up, like a lift in a building, and there's lots of space through the needles for a view at the top. That makes up for the scratches. Pine trees have bald, sticky-out bits that claw at your legs as you move higher. A couple of times, the cricket bag got caught on the spikes. I put it on my front for the hardest part of the climb, up high where the branches thickened and swayed like dancers when the wind blew.

When I could go no further, I wedged my feet in some branches each side of the trunk. I must have been three stories up. Chapman Street was a line of shining corrugated iron rooftops, dotted with green and brown patchwork lawns. Straight down, through criss-crossed branches, was a chestnut carpet of dried needles and dead bracken.

I took off the bag and gripped it between my knees to undo the zip. I held the cloak tightly when I shook it out. I draped it round my shoulders, then I tied it together at the base of my neck. When I pulled myself up to standing, I was completely transformed.

It must have been five o'clock when I saw the car coming into the village. I knew straight away that it was Mrs Parata because no one else had a convertible like hers. The sun was getting lower in the sky, coming in sideways to where I was perched. It burnt through rich green needles onto the surface of the cloak, making it darker, like rust. It shone on Mrs Parata, too. Her dress looked as purple as Mrs Sullivan's lupins.

She walked up the steps to my house and knocked on the door. Then she went along the side of the house and peered in the windows, shading her eyes with her hand. She went out of sight for a while, then she came tearing around from the back, faster than I'd ever thought she could move. Across she went to Mrs Sullivan's house and started bashing on her door. Then Mrs Sullivan came out, all agitated. They both went inside, and then they both came out again and ran across the road to the back of my house. I heard a faint sound of glass smashing and it all went very quiet, except for the whispering of the sea through the treetops.

About ten minutes later, a big vehicle came humming along the road. It didn't have a siren – just flashing red lights – which made it seem like I was watching a movie with the sound turned off. Mrs Sullivan had her hands over her face and someone brought a white plastic chair onto her lime-green lawn. She sat down on it and I thought about the dents it would make in the grass.

I stopped watching when the men started moving out of my house. By then, the sun was really coming in hard at me, so I pulled myself down into the cloak; like when a bird rests its head right back into its feathers and it looks like it's asleep. When I came back out, the sun had moved round and the vehicles had all left, except for one lady in a uniform, who stood by the fence with Mrs Sullivan and Mrs Parata. Mrs Sullivan was pointing down the road to the bus stop, then she pointed over at the pines.

Mrs Parata walked across the road and stood at the edge of the plantation.

"Marama," she called. "Marama! Are you in there?"

She came a little further in. Her purple dress swished past needles, scratched on twigs.

"Marama?" She was right at the trunk of my tree. "Marama, is that you?" She looked straight up at me.

"I'm a bird," I said.

"I know," she said.

"I'm sending her a message," I said. "I'm communicating."

She craned her head back.

"Marama," she said. "I understand. But you can come down now."

I put the cloak back in the bag and climbed down. I found Mrs Parata sitting on a wide-spreading branch, looking a bit crumpled.

"Look," I said, holding up the front of the cloak. "It's ruined."

She squinted hard at it. I guess the stain had dried since lunchtime, and it had faded, too. The signature feathers still looked special.

Mrs Parata put an arm around my shoulder.

"It's a strong cloak, Marama," she said.

She took it from me and we walked back to the edge of the pines.

"We need to know if you have any whānau," she said. "Do you know what that means?"

Of course I knew. We'd talked about it in class.

"There's Tama," I said. "But I haven't seen him in a few days."

I sat on Mrs Sullivan's lawn while Mrs Parata talked to the police lady. Then she came over and said I'd be staying at her place that night. She helped me collect some things from the house. I said goodbye to Mrs Sullivan while Mrs Parata put my bag in the boot of her car. The top was still down and when I went around to the passenger side, the cloak was spread out across the cream leather. She took it off the seat, and she put it around my shoulders.

I got into the car and we set off down Chapman Street in the little green convertible; Mrs Parata's hair sitting stiff and high off her forehead, me on the passenger side, a blaze of red and scarlet, rustling with the spirits of seventy kaka birds. Just like that, I flew all the way back to town.

Abhishek Sengupta

Abhishek Sengupta is imaginary. Mostly, people would want to believe he uses magical realism to write novels about world issues, even though he is stuck inside a window in Kolkata, India, but he knows none of it is true. He doesn't exist. Only his imaginary writing does and has appeared in some periodicals and anthologies around the globe, won a few prizes, and been published alongside the likes of Neil Gaiman (who is a little less imaginary). If you're gifted, however, you may imagine him on Twitter @AbhishekSWrites.

THINGS TO DO
ON THE EVE OF
YOUR KILLING

For Your Father, Who Still Thinks Yesterday and Tomorrow are the Same Things

- Pluck two constellations. Any two. (Your choice.) Arrange them on the ceiling of your father's room such that they faced each other every yesterday and will face away from each other every tomorrow. Now ask him to look at it today. When his eyes water and he says he can't see the constellations clearly even with his glasses on, tell him he isn't trying hard enough. Tell him he's stopped trying for a long time now. Tell him that if there's anything that makes you happy about what's to come, it's that you'll never have to see his face again.
- When he throws his paperweight at you, duck. Or don't. (Your choice.) But think of the mother duck and the ducklings in the pond outside the courtyard of your home. Think of them

swimming in a line, the mother duck cutting the sun in the water right down the middle and the ducklings using that opening to dip straight into the darkness and beyond and never coming out, only their vestiges following the mother duck who believes that one day she'll find the end of the pond that leads to the river where the kingdom of swans begins and she'll urge her ducklings to go swim on their own. Feel the anger bubble inside you at the mother duck's stupidity. Blame your father for your mother's early demise. Shout at him. Or don't.

• Press your handkerchief at the spot on your forehead where it's bleeding now if you hadn't ducked in the previous step. (If you ducked, skip to the next step.) Your father who can't see the constellations on the ceiling properly never misses your forehead when throwing his paperweight at you. You call that animal instinct. He calls it a lesson for the years to come. Fight the urge to hold him by the collar and shake him hard, the urge to remind him that there are no years to come for you. Yes, fight that urge. (Not a matter of choice this time.) Your old man is too frail, and you could easily break him by that simple act of shaking him like a bottle of medicine, by reminding him what day tomorrow is supposed to be. It's best that at least one of you remain unbroken by tomorrow. But make sure you're not thinking aloud; otherwise, he'll correct you, saying that if you were okay yesterday, you'd naturally be okay tomorrow as well, because yesterday and tomorrow mirror each other.

• When your wife opens the door behind you and steps inside with two cups of tea, step aside. Let her pass and let her place the first cup of tea on your father's bedside table. Hold no grudges for your father getting preferential treatment. Let her pick up the paperweight from the floor and place the weapon in its usual place on the same bedside table beside the tea, ready to be picked up and hurled at you once again at the smallest provocation. Hold no grudges against your wife for making it possible. Instead, concentrate on the light pink salwar she's wearing with the rose red dupatta. Watch as her mehndi-painted hands push behind her ear that single strand of hair that had fallen in front of her eyes. Watch her smile softly at you, her lips pressed, watching you watch her as she steps out of the room, and sense your heart melt for the umpteenth time. Wish that God had made her less beautiful than this.

- With your wife gone and your heart beating faster than usual, step closer to your father's bed. Sit. Yes, place yourself on one side of the bed. Overcome your reluctance, if required. Now watch your father carefully. Or if you're uncomfortable staring at him for too long, watch the cup of tea your wife has brought for him. (You'll get the same result, no matter which you choose.) Be aware of the storm in the teacup. Be aware of the frenzied winds that are swishing inside the room. Your father doesn't see the wind nor hear it. But you do. You both see and hear the catastrophe lying in wait, outside the boundary walls of your courtyard, waiting for the right time to pay its visit and tear down a splintered future. Be aware this is the last night. Take your father's hand in yours. Put it to your temple. Or bring your temple down to the back of his hand. (Your choice.) Then, sob as soundlessly as your mother used to.

For Your Mother-in-Law, Who Stays with Your Family and Strays into Their Minds.

- Sprinkle water on the Bliss you plucked from the garden. Make sure its transparent petals are shiny and bright. If its green curiosity runs a little too long, trim it to fit the size of your palm. Or better still, the size of your mother-in-law's palm. Then, present it to her. If she cries, tell her you're only keeping your promise – the one in which you had pledged to bring her Bliss only after you had fulfilled her wish. If she cries a little more at that, remind her she's the closest thing you have to a mother and you had to do this much for her daughter, anyway, because you love her no less than she does. And if she's still crying after that, put an arm around her shoulder (preferably your right one because she's superstitious), and explain to her the things she'll need to take care of after you're gone.

- When your wife steps into this room (but not with cups of tea) and asks you why you're stealing her mother's love and commands you to scoot, move over to make space for her to sit between you and your mother-in-law. Hold no grudges if she puts her head on her mother's shoulder instead of yours. (She has one head only.) Take in the sandalwood aroma of her skin and the lavender fragrance of her hair, and take her hand in yours, your fingers between hers. Let go of her hand only when your five-year-old son calls your wife from the other room. After she leaves, sit quietly. Make sure both you and your mother-in-law don't speak for the next five minutes or so. In this interval, feel free to sigh as many times as you wish.

- Pay attention to your mother-in-law's words when she claims she dreamt her way into your mother's mind last night. Ask your mother-in-law what she found there. When she tells you your mother is very impressed with the brave face Potai puts on all the time these days, get up from the bed and begin pacing about the room. Potai, as you of course remember, is the nickname your mother had given you. But because only she used to call you that, the name fell into disuse after she passed away. Now, the resurfacing of that name reminds you of the time when you were yet too little to understand why some nights your mother wore her costliest saris and your father opened the door for her, to let her disappear into the darkness. Later, when you were a little wiser, you asked your father why she had to go to the *zamindar bari,* the house of the landlords, at night, and your father said it was so that all of you could stay here and stay alive. Later still, you remember leaping to your mother's feet, clutching onto her leg, and your father pulling you away, and you screaming at the top of your voice, and yet your mother not looking behind, walking out of the courtyard as briskly as possible for yet another night.

- Tell your mother-in-law that your father is a coward, has been so all his life, but he's also very lonely, has never stepped out of the house ever since your mother passed away, never had a friend since. When your mother-in-law shakes her head, anticipating what's coming, and says she's tried but cannot dream her way into his mind because there's a thick cluster of cacti inside, you have two choices. You may ask her to replace the cacti with freshly planted shoots of Bliss from your garden, replace the brown thorns with green curiosity, replace fear with empathy, so he may breathe once again. That pathetic coward needs to breathe! Or you can ask your mother-in-law not to dream her way into his mind at all, but step into his room in person, drink the cup of tea her daughter has served for your father but which he never touches, and tell him about her own escapades into your mother's mind. (If you're taking this route, warn your mother-in-law about the paperweight. Alternatively, teach her to duck.) Convince her to keep telling him about your mother's mind until he begins trusting her as much as he trusted your mother and becomes as sure of your mother-in-law's good intentions as he was about the fact that your mother never loved any man other than him, even up to the last day of her life, even though the last word she had uttered was strangely garbled, and it didn't sound like his name, nor Potai's.

• Above all, don't forget to remind your mother-in-law to be a good grandma, even when she describes the candle inside your son's mind – one that keeps flickering in a breeze that blows from the darkness. She must never let that candle extinguish no matter how strong the breeze is because that's what a grandma does. Instead, tomorrow after they've beaten you numb, held you by your hair, and dragged you out of the courtyard like a stack of hay to hack you, she must shut the main door to the courtyard, bolt it from the inside, so that even when the catastrophe hits, the door is not flung open by a gust of wind and the candle stays aglow. Teach her how to close the narrow opening under the door with stacks of old clothes, so the pool of blood never crosses the threshold and seeps into the courtyard; otherwise, they'll need to wash it meticulously, over and over again, until all stains are gone.

For Your Son, Who Says Red Doesn't Exist and Green is Just Another Name for Envy

• Before you step into your son's room, remember that the last time you had plucked a hair off your arm, he had screamed as if your arm was his. You were only trying to frighten him and hadn't wanted to succeed so brazenly. But he had run out of his room and kept shrieking in the courtyard, frightening away the crows and the sparrows and the mice and the cockroaches, and it had taken that angelic woman who happens to be your wife to pull him in her arms and make him stop. Remember how you had concluded that day that your son was all wrongly wired. Remember how, on the very same day, you had approached your son from behind, with your upper teeth biting your lower lip, as you sneakily targeted the top of your son's head for a four-fingered slap out of the blue, and him giggling and looking up at you instead of weeping in pain, then throwing both his hands up in the air. He wanted to be carried on your shoulder. When they take you, they'll take your shoulders away from him. No rides afterwards.

- Tonight, pick up the various memories scattered all over the floor, haphazardly, as you find your son has already fallen asleep. Put those memories on their respective shelves, in the order your wife does, so they make sense sequentially. Memories filed non-sequentially is madness. There's no room for madness here. Know you have to wake your son up from his sleep. Be in no two minds about that. If you don't, he'll never know you returned this evening and would assume you disappeared a day before you actually did. Dates are important because memories filed non-sequentially is madness.

- Once your son has opened his eyes, tell him one last made-up bedtime story to keep him awake. In it, a yeti living in the Himalayas goes searching for a peace he has lost. He braves the harsh cold, the blizzards, and the steep cliffs with an undying hope and vigour. At last, he smells his peace and follows the scent to a den in which a pack of wolves reside. They refuse to hand him over the peace. It's theirs now, they say. The yeti doesn't want to fight for his peace. He says they best come to an agreement; he would give them something in return for his peace. There's a shawl he kept from a human who died in the mountains. He could give it to them. The wolves agree to return his peace if he brought that shawl to them. So, the yeti braves the harsh cold, the blizzards, and the steep cliffs once again and goes all the way back to his own cave, retrieves the shawl, and returns through the same challenges. But on reaching the wolves' den, he finds they have already devoured his peace, the last remnants of that peace twinkling in their teeth. So, the yeti goes on a rampage. He kills every wolf in there, yet his peace is gone. He heaps the carcasses together, covers them with the shawl he brought them, and leaves. While you're telling your son that story, make sure he's awake at all times. If he appears drowsy, finger-flick him on his head. It's important that he listens. That story is all he'll have when he's old enough to understand.

- Ask him not to step out of his room tomorrow. Be thankful that because he's colourblind, the hue of blood he sees is not as stark as it is for the rest of you. He could easily mistake it for something else, like tree sap or wastewater from one of the drains. Still, know it's best that he does not ask questions and someone needs to lie to him, to save his flame from extinguishing.

- If he asks whether his mother will keep putting him to sleep with a lullaby every night (and he most probably *will* bring up that question), ask him instead if that's not how he fell asleep tonight as well before you came to awaken him again. And when he nods, kiss him on the forehead, tell him that she'll always be around for him, as long as he needs her. If he smiles at that, flick his nose with your index finger and smile with him. If he tears up on being kissed, pull him into an embrace and hold him there until you feel the flame inside him has stopped dancing in the wind that blows from the darkness.

For Your Wife, Who'll Never Believe That You Won't Still be Around in These Courtyards

- Pluck two more constellations from the dark skies above, one more Bliss from your garden, and another hair off your arm and hope your wife believes that your imminent death is real and that you may not linger around after that. When she returns to your room after completing her daily chores, sits in her favourite chair, and resumes knitting the sweater for you, for the coming winter, look away. You may not want to, but still, you must. Then tell her you're sorry. You're sorry for leaving to work at the fields that day even after she said she sensed something was amiss in the air, that you'd better stay by her side that day, that she was afraid something might happen to her, and you laughed it off, kissed her on the forehead, called her a crazy woman and left. Do you remember how you believed then that even though you were still a tenant farmer like your father was, the times had changed? That your wife would never have to set foot inside the gates your mother did? Curse yourself. Yes, it helps at times. Go ahead. Curse yourself.
- A corpse must always look beautiful, no matter what it must have gone through in its lifetime. Did you ever read about desairologists – the professionally qualified cosmetologists who make your deceased kins look beautiful? Such professionals may not exist in this country, or you may have been a little too poor to call for their services, but know that you're in the right if you wished your wife to look beautiful when, a week ago, her corpse was brought

into your courtyard by the *zamindar's* servants as a nice gesture of civility. Are those servants the same people who took her too, the other day, against her will? Ask that question to yourself. (But you'll never find an answer.) Rather, try to remember how you focussed on your wife's corpse, that day, and wished that she had appeared more peaceful, at least, in her death. She had looked peaceful all her life, so why not as a corpse? But with her, they had stolen your greatest source of peace, and it's not something you easily forget. Not something you easily forgive. So, go and sit on the floor where your wife is busy knitting the sweater and apologise to her for the things you have done, for being so reckless and not thinking about your son who is about to lose his father too tomorrow. Watch her brush your comment away, and say that you're not going anywhere, after all, isn't she still around even now?

• Make her happy by telling her that you fulfilled her mother's wish by plucking each of those lecherous wolves who had laid their dirty hands on her, not only out of their luxurious mansion but off the face of this Earth. Know that a woman is happier when you've done something for her mother than she is if you brought her a costly present. But then also tell her you did today not only what you had promised to her mother but what you had to do to bring your wife justice and that you don't care what they do to you tomorrow because you're not a coward. If she smiles at that last part of your statement, repeat that you're not a coward. If she nods her head this time, don't feel like you've been given a consolation prize. Instead, ask her if she'd sing the same lullaby she sang for your son.

• Put your head on her lap and let her run her fingers through your hair as she sings for you. It's a lullaby about a mother putting her child to sleep. What did you expect? There are no lullabies for husbands. Make do with what you have. Now, with your eyes closed, concentrate on the soft, cottony things that land on your skin. Those are peace raining from the skies. If you were to play a cosmic rock-paper-scissors, what would a paperweight, a candle, and a sweater do to each other? Think hard about that. You've got to get the sequence right, because memories shelved non-sequentially is madness, and there's no room left in this house for any more madness.

Mahsuda Snaith

After the release of her debut novel, *The Things We Thought We Knew*, Mahsuda Snaith was named an 'Observer New Face of Fiction' and was chosen as a World Book Night writer in 2019. Her second novel, *How to Find Home*, was chosen as a BBC Radio 4 'Book at Bedtime'. She is the winner of the 2014 SI Leeds Literary Prize and 2014 Bristol Short Story Prize. Mahsuda has led creative writing workshops in universities, hospitals, schools and a homeless hostel, been a mentor for a variety of writing organisations and was a judge for the 2021 Bristol Short Story Prize. She is a commissioned writer for the Colonial Countryside project and her short story, *The Panther's Tale*, is included in *Hag: Forgotten Folktales Retold*. Mahsuda works as a writing coach at The Novelry. Find out more at www.mahsudasnaith.com.

THE ART OF FLOOD SURVIVAL

The flood comes overnight. I hear the *phlunkk! phlunnk!* as feet hit water. The English scream. Aiyh! Their voices clatter and slap my ears.

"It does not flood in Syhlet," Mahmud told them. He had leant back on his chair, balancing his fat body on two legs as he stuffed paan leaf in the cave of his cheek. "We people have the sense to live on higher ground."

Sense. Aiyh! As if floods have knowledge of such things. In the village of my birth we did not live on lower ground because we had no sense, we lived there because we had no choice. We learnt to survive the floods, to tie boats to iron posts, to build raised platforms for livestock. We made portable ovens to keep us fed in the worst of conditions and scaled the wire trunks of palm trees, keeping clear of danger while assessing the damage. Water can drown you but, if you give into its force, it can also keep you afloat.

But the English, they have no survival skills. They holler through the blue-black night even though it will make no difference. Even though this is Bangladesh, where screaming for help is as fruitful as asking the monsoon to stop bringing rain...

It is early morning when they arrive. The baby-taxi screeches a honking tune that cuts through the noise of the green rainfall. When we reach the gate the English are already outside. The girls are dressed in Western clothes; t-shirts and jeans like the boys in town but cut in a way that clings to the thighs. Their skin is a watery mud colour that makes them look sickly. The mother wears a salwar kameez; white scarf wrapped over her head, knot beneath her chin. You can hear the Bengali in the way she sighs but her body is wound up tight like a coiled rattlesnake.

There is no father with them. I wait a moment but when the taxi driver brings the last suitcase there is still no one.

"Rabeya!" cries Auntie snapping her hand towards the gate.

The rain smacks my face as I push the bars shut. When I run inside I stand behind the screen door where the English will not see me.

"Crazy crazy!" the mother is wailing.

She slaps her head, dropping down on Uncle's rosewood chair. Her round body deflates as she tells Auntie of the beggars at the airport, how they grabbed for their suitcases, had pulled at their clothes. They were mobbed she says, and nobody tells her she has forgotten her country already. That there is no mobbing in Bangladesh; just life.

Auntie tells me to tend to the chai in the kitchen. It has been brewing in a large steel pan with the lime green of cardamom pods and the deep mahogany of cloves and cinnamon floating on top. I sweeten it with four heaped spoons of sugar, stirring slowly as I add milk. The fiery smell hits the air, covering the sour stench of the rubbish heap in the back yard. When Auntie walks in she stops, chest inflating.

They are not my real Auntie and Uncle; they are my masters but they still let me call them this. Zubaida says this makes them good people. In her house they cry out 'Girl! Bring me the newspaper! Girl! Sweep the floors!' They treat her as if she is nothing more than an animal in the yard. Aiyh! No better than a dog on the street.

I ladle the chai into the teacups. They are white porcelain with pink roses and gold trim on the handles. I place them carefully across a steel tray. Auntie's hands shake as she lifts it, cups tinkling against the steel. I hope the guests will think this is because of age and not because she is worried about Mahmud arriving home earlier than Uncle.

I stay in the kitchen, turning the heat low beneath the pan, hearing the loud chatter of the two ladies as they reminisce about their childhood.

"*Rabeya!*" Auntie cries.

When I run into the main room, the English girls are limp on their seats. Their mud-water faces are now gaunt as goats as they swot lazily at clammy skin.

"*Coils*," Auntie says.

I run to get the coils, placing them around the room before lighting the ends of their spiralling bodies. Smoke ripples up from their amber tails, spreading out into a fountain as it hits the ceiling. I watch the mosquitos fly into the fog before stumbling out. Their whining buzz clips to an end. If I had the power I would kill every mosquito in Bangladesh! With one flick of my hand I would shatter their needle mouths and burst their blood-filled bodies. Such tiny creatures yet still they are the greatest flood survivors of them all.

"Assalam alaikum."

I turn to see Uncle in the doorway. He stands in his long white kurta like the Great Egret standing in the tall grass of the paddy fields. There is much noise and touching of feet. Even the English girls show this respect. I run to the kitchen to bring out another cup of chai. When I come back Auntie passes it to Uncle, lifting the teacup by the saucer, hands no longer shaking.

Auntie tells me to sweep the girls' room. When I go in they are sitting on the bed, backs slumped against the brick. The younger girl is touching the screen of a thin silver box.

I try to be invisible to them because I do not want them to slap me the way Mahmud does. Auntie's slaps are short and sharp but Mahmud thumps so hard it makes me dizzy.

"What is your name?" asks one of the girls.

It is the older one. Her Bengali is weak but I do not tell her this.

"Rabeya," I say, staying squat to the floor.

I sweep the dust with a straw broom while the girl questions me. Where am I from? Where is my family? What are my jobs? Do I mind this work?

She speaks these questions with an easy smile and I think perhaps she is tricking me; that she will report me to Uncle. I tell her I am from a small village many miles outside of Syhlet. I have four sisters and two brothers.

"When do you see them?"

I pause, watching the straw twist side to side as I sweep.

"Before the last monsoon, maybe longer."

The younger girl looks up from her box. She says something but, aiyh!, her Bengali is worse than her sisters. I thought these English were well educated but they cannot even speak their own language.

"She's asking if you miss them," the older one says.

I stop sweeping. I think about my baby brothers and how I carried them around the village like monkeys carry their young. I think of Zubaida, just one year older than me, and how she hollered when she had to return to her master's house. How she clung onto my arm as

Abba pulled her to the rickshaw, wailing and shouting my name as if it was me who decided she should go. Abba grabbed hold of her hair and yanked so hard she had no choice but to let go. I ran inside with tears in my eyes to find Amma plucking the feathers off a dead duck. She did not look up but simply wiped the sweat from her forehead.

"No," I say. "I do not miss them."

I think this will be the end of it but the girl now asks my age. I shrug. When I do this the younger one leans closer to her sister and whispers in her ear.

"My sister thinks you are eight or nine," the older one says.

I think of the charity school in the village and how they taught us numbers, pushing pink chalk in large loops across slate, singing the sequence out loud.

"Eight," I say. "Yes I am eight."

The girls are quiet. I leave the room quickly before they think of more questions.

I help Auntie gut the ilish fish and fetch the heavy pots into the kitchen. I am small but I am strong and lift two or three pots, no problem. Aiyh! I am probably stronger than a boy!

Auntie takes the edge of her knife and skims the scales off the fish in one straight sweep. The small discs shimmer as they make a silver-pink pile on the floor. I look at the goggling eyes of the ilish, wondering if it saw the net before the fishermen caught it.

There is a clatter at the front gate. For a moment I think it is Uncle returning from the masjid, but then I hear the rev of a motorbike.

Auntie's face tightens as she looks at me.

"Chai."

I run over to the steel pan, tilting it over as I scoop out what is left.

When I walk into the main room Mahmud is sitting on a chair with legs spread wide, thumbs hooked into pockets. His black moustache is waxed into points like a film villain. Mahmud preens and combs his moustache every day. I believe the closest he feels to love is his adoration of that gleaming cockroach.

"Of course my dear cousins," he says as I bring him the chai. "It is so good to see you."

He wiggles his head and gives them his phann stained grin, leaving me to stand with the teacup in my hand. The mother is wearing a leaf green sari. She sits in her chair, body loose with the heat. The girls are fatigued and do not look at their cousin. I think this makes them wise.

Auntie walks in and suddenly Mamud's voice grows loud.

"How are you liking our great country of Bangladesh?"

The girl's nod but do not smile while their mother fans her face with a newspaper. I see Auntie's brow wrinkle. She wants to reprimand Mahmud for his lateness but instead mops the sweat from her forehead with the end of her sari.

"They have not left the house yet," she says.

Mahmud's eyes widen as though she has told him they have not eaten for three days.

"This is terrible!" he cries. "Bangladesh is the most beautiful country in all of Asia! Our tea plantations are very famous. Of course your cousin Mahmud will take you."

The girls' eyes lift while Auntie's become hard.

"They are here for business only. There is no point dragging them around during monsoon."

Mahmud grins at his cousins.

"What is the point of business if there is no *pleasure*."

The girls look at each other, then lower their heads.

Mahmud's phone buzzes and he leaves the room. When he returns he is wiggling his head and grinning.

"I have spoken to my friend. We will go to the plantation tomorrow. It will be very cheap."

Auntie begins to protest but the mother stops her.

"He is right," she says. "My children should see the beauty of our country."

When Auntie marches back into the kitchen Mahmud sits down. He swings back on the chair.

"How are you liking your cousin Mahmud and his moustache?"

He twiddles the ends of his whiskers. They all laugh.

The next day the girls put on a salwar kameez and cover their heads with their dupattas. Even still, the taxi driver will see their easy smiles and treble the rates.

The older one smiles at me as I sweep the room, but I look away. She comes to me, placing a finger on my chin, and turns my face to look at her. For a moment I think she will slap me but instead she whispers.

"You must not be sad. We shall bring back photos."

I do not understand this word.

"*Foh-toe?*" I say.

She takes out a red box from her bag and holds it in front of her. When she presses the button a light pops from the corner. She turns the box around and, aiyh!, I see my face looking back at me with surprise.

"I am inside?" I ask, tapping the screen.

"No no," says the older sister. "It is just a photo."

"*Foh-toe.*"

She laughs and I laugh too. The other sister seems pleased and joins in. Mahmud hears all this cheerfulness and is quick to investigate.

When he strides in I squat low and begin to sweep. I glance up as he takes hold of the box and twiddles his moustache.

"Yar yar, this is a very good camera."

He looks it over as though he is an expert when all he has is a mobile phone, not slim and silver like the girls, but thick and black like a sun-scorched cow turd. He sees me scowling at him and, even though I know he wants to slap me, he grins at his cousins and tells them the baby taxis have arrived.

I watch them leave through the bars of the gate. The rain is light but the girls carry big umbrellas until they are inside the vehicles. Mahmud holds his arm out for the mother and sweet-talks her all the way to the baby taxi. I look down the street at the bougainvillea trailing over white painted walls, stray dogs lying lazy in the sun, school children riding their bikes through rust coloured mud. I lock the padlock on the gate. When I look up I see the girls waving from the baby taxi. It is only when I look behind me that I realise they are waving at me.

As I squat to wash the dishes I think of the children riding home from school. The boys in their shorts and shirts, the girls wearing pinafore dresses, hair oiled and plaited in black ropes on either side of their head. The water bubbles as it hits the stone and I carry on scrubbing until every fishbone is washed down the drain.

The lady from the charity wanted me to go to a school here in Syhlet. She came to the house and cupped her hand around my cheek, asking me questions about what village I came from. I wanted to tell her about the charity school back home, how they taught me to read and write and how I was always top of my class! But I knew that I could not say these things in front of Uncle. So he spoke for me instead, chin raised high as though insulted to be asked in the first place.

Later I heard Mahmud tell Uncle there was no use educating a child who would only be a housegirl. He tossed his hand in the air.

"It will give her airs and graces," he said.

Uncle listened and, for the first time I have witnessed, agreed with Mahmud. Uncle is older than me and wiser but, aiyh! I wish he had not.

Zubaida told me of a housegirl, just like us, who attended a charity school and learnt art, dancing, reading and writing. This same girl went to her master asking for more pay because she was now a skilled worker. I asked Zubaida if she was beaten badly for this but Zubaida said no.

"He agreed! Can you believe it Rabeya?"

Aiyh! I could not.

I did not fight and kick the day I was sent here to work, but I cried so wildly that everyone stopped their street work to look at us. When we were outside the house Abba grabbed hold of me, telling me he would beat me if I carried on with my wailing. I should be grateful, he said, the money I would send home would feed the whole family. Wasn't this better than being dumped on the streets and left to beg for my living? Or being married off to a fifty-year-old man who would treat me like a slave and worse besides? I should be grateful for this job and respect my employees or they would kick me out. I must not tell them I could read and write or they would think me too educated. It was better that I appeared stupid to them.

So I hid this from my masters and they have been happy with my stupidity. It is like Mahmud says, there is no use educating a child who will only be a housegirl.

The sky is sapphire-black when Mahmud and the English return. They walk through the gate with wide grins and a rumbling laughter that echoes through the rain. When they are inside I see the mother search through her purse and place taka notes in Mahmud's hand. He protests, but only for a moment.

Later, the girls usher me to their room.

"Look," says the older girl, holding her photobox in front of me.

On the screen I see pictures of green hills rolling out for miles, ladies carrying woven baskets filled with freshly picked leaves on their heads. I ask the girls if they saw tigers. Their eyes widen and they say *nooo!*

Our talking stops when we hear Mahmud shouting from the main room.

"Allah!" he cries. "You cannot expect things to be easy like England. Your papers will be lost, they will charge you twice the fee!"

We hear the mumble of the mother's voice.

"Trust me auntie!" Mahmud says. "I know people who can help with this problem. It will take one day, maximum."

Mahmud does not return for three days.

The mother begins to complain about the heat and her back pain, pacing the house up and down. When she speaks with Uncle and Auntie she is tense, her words sharp. Even her daughters are afraid, sneaking off to their room to whisper in words I cannot understand.

They no longer speak to me. I forgive them for this because, when the time comes, I know they will help me.

When Mahmud returns it is after nightfall. He is wet with rain and stinks of beer. He makes so much noise singing and banging into furniture that everyone stumbles out of their beds. I follow the girls as they step into the main room, staying crouched down in the corner so he cannot see me. Since the other children married and left, Uncle has controlled his son single-handedly but even he cannot tame a drunk Mahmud.

"You must not worry," Mahmud tells the mother. "You will get your money back twofold. You must give me time, yar?"

"I want it now!" she says, slapping her hands together. "We have airplane seats booked for tomorrow."

Mahmud shrugs his shoulders.

"I will forward you the money."

He lifts his hand as though this is the end of the matter.

Auntie steps forward. The moonlight hits her eyes and I see they are wide, red lines weaving through the white. She begins chopping her hand towards Mahmud.

"Fool boy! You have gambled it away! You have drunk it down the drain! You are a devil boy Mahmud and one of these days you will be killed for your sins!"

Mahmud's eyes grow as wide as his mother's. He stands straight, his top lip curling back beneath his cockroach moustache.

"You will ruin my name old woman?"

His voice creeps higher with each word.

"You will make a fool of me in front of my English relatives?!"

Mahmud swings his hand up. His eyes are so fierce that I know the blow will send Auntie to the floor.

"Aiyh!" Uncle cries.

The noise is enough to keep Mahmud's hand hovering in the air.

When Uncle speaks again his voice is dry and rattling.

"Do not bring any more shame on this house Mahmud," he says. "Allah knows I will not allow it!"

Mahmud looks at his father, then at his English cousins who have horror flickering through their eyes. He turns to go, the clattering of the gate soon followed by the rev of his motorbike.

The girls toss on their mattress and cannot sleep. I creep to the side of their bed, hooking my fingers on the edge of their sheets.

"You are going back to England tomorrow?"

For a while, all I hear is the rain beating on the roof and the howling of wind.

"Yes."

It is the older one that speaks. I see the roundness of her cheek glow in the soft moonlight. I squeeze on tighter to the sheets, feeling the moth-eaten holes between my fingers.

"Will you take me?"

The rain goes *da-rum, da-rum* inside me, filling me up like a barrel. I wait, wondering if she has not heard.

"I shall be a very good servant," I say.

Her body curls tight, sheets rippling around her legs.

"We do not have servants in England."

I frown and look back at her cheek.

"Will you take me anyway?"

The wind howls like a tortured banshee. I watch her jaw clench and think it is from fear, but when she speaks again her voice is stern and sharp.

"No Rabeya. Now please leave us alone."

…The flood comes overnight. When the waters rise I tie the skirt of my kameez around my waist and climb out of the back window.

As the English scream and Auntie and Uncle try to make sense of the flood I scramble up the trunk of a starfruit tree. I hear Auntie calling all the names of her children until Uncle reminds her it is only Mahmud who lives with them now.

"Mahmud!" she cries. "Where is my dear boy Mahmud?"

She carries on calling his name even when they are through the gate, the English following in a neat line as they wade through the water.

She does not call for me. But then, I did not expect her to.

I pull a starfruit from the branch of the tree and bite into its rubbery skin. The flesh is sweet and fragrant. Soon, the noise of Auntie's wailing fades, replaced with the drumming of rainfall. She thinks her son has perished in the waters but Mahmud is a mosquito. He will profit from this flood just like those biting beasts do; making love to the still water, laying their eggs within. As the water rises so will his numbers, a thousand little Mahmud's swarming for the nearest prey.

I watch the sun rise over the flooded city. The red shimmers across the water like flames in a rubbish pyre. Far away I see men in lungis riding rickshaws and the bare chests of boys as they wash themselves from the waist up. I look over the pastel painted houses and palm trees shooting up to the sky and think this must be what the Great Egret sees when she is flying to her next destination. I will be like the bird; I will fly from this place, the wind rushing through my feathers with wings outstretched.

I hear the rumble of an engine. When I rub my eyes I see an orange rescue boat cutting through the water. A rippled tail fans out from behind. There is an art to flood survival. The art is to prosper from it. I shout at the boat, my cries so loud that the men look up and cut their engine dead.

As I climb down the trunk I think of my story.

I will tell them I am from a good family, washed away in the floods.

I will tell them I am well educated, that I know how to read and write.

I will tell them I am a survivor.

Cameron Stewart

Cameron Stewart is a writer based in Sydney, Australia. He grew up on a farm near Mullumbimby, by way of Alice Springs, Canberra and Cairns. Diversity of place informs much of his writing as does an interest in flawed characters trying to do their best. Cameron holds an MA (Creative Writing) from the University of Technology, Sydney and a BA (Performing Arts) from the University of Western Sydney (Theatre Nepean). Cameron is an award winning, short fiction writer and has been published in Australia, the UK and the USA. His debut novel, *Why Do Horses Run?* is being released by Allen & Unwin in April 2024. He is currently working on his second novel, *Cosmonaut*.

BLACK SNOW

few miles out of town on a dirt road in bushland, my father pulled over and parked in a shallow ditch. 'Stay in the car,' he threw at me over his shoulder. Doors opened and closed, and he and Leah walked off with a blanket and a clinking bag of bottles. Leah was my father's girlfriend. She looked after me when he worked in the mines, but now he was home for good. I locked the doors and pulled out a book my uncle gave me for my birthday. It was about a man and a boy walking around in the cold trying to avoid people who wanted to eat them. What kind of present is that? I prefer to read something real, like science. Threads of sunlight filtered through shifting trees and angled into the cabin. A logging truck rumbled by, pluming dust. Hours passed. It was autumn in Tasmania, and the sun dropped like a shot duck. There was an old towel in the back which I threw over my shoulders for warmth. My toes felt like pebbles in cold river water. Tracing patterns on the leather seats, I picked at some broken stitching. In the glovebox, I found papers, chewed pens, lipstick, a few coins – and a butter knife.

'Why did you do it?' my father yelled at me later. 'Why the fuck did you do it? Is there something wrong with your head?'

I asked him if there was something wrong with his head.

'Watch your mouth,' he said, 'or I'll knock your block off.'

Leah told him to take it easy.

'Should make the little cunt walk,' said my father.

I wished he'd just hit me and be done with it. If pressed, I'd say that the popping sound the butter knife made as I punched it through the leather made me feel good. I knew what I was doing was wrong and at first thought I'd only stab one hole, a hole that wouldn't be noticed, but once I got started I couldn't stop.

South of the tropical city of Cairns, a violent updraft rushed five thousand feet up the steep ridge of the mountain. Rainforest and a summit strewn with granite boulders stood shrouded in mist and rain. As the plane shuddered through a column of swirling, black cloud, and yawed east towards the sea, I wondered why I was being sent to stay with my uncle at the other end of the country. Water droplets shimmered and flicked across my window like shattered beads of mercury. The fuselage vibrated in buffeting wind and a lone, green light blinked on the wingtip. There was no hand to hold. Suddenly the aircraft dropped into blinding light. Into sunshine. Into safety. I surveyed paddocks of wet sugar cane that gridded the earth.

The first thing that struck me, stepping off the plane, was the tropical air. Beyond the heat and jet fuel were smells hard to identify, smells I'd soon be steeped in – damp earth and molasses, mangoes and diesel, papayas, compost and custard apples, burnt sugar and stale beer. Burning cane. Approaching thunderstorms. Ash.

Uncle John was waiting in the arrivals lounge – legs smeared in mud. Shoeless. A scar ran from cheekbone to lip making him look mean.

'You caught me in the middle of something,' he said as we walked to his dented Landrover. Heat rose off the bitumen carpark.

'Might want to lose the jacket and the jeans,' he added. 'And the shoes.'

Half an hour later we waded barefoot across the mudflats of the Cairns esplanade, shin deep in stinking mud. I struggled to keep up. The tide was low, and we headed out a fair way. Uncle John pointed out birds I'd never heard of – spoonbills, plovers, knots and curlews.

'See that little one?' he said, pointing to a group of seabirds feeding on the mud. He handed me his binoculars. I recognised a pelican.

'To the left of that,' he said. 'Tiny one with black legs and a black bill. Mottled on top. White underneath.'

'Yeah, I see it.'

'It's a red-necked stint.'

Don't know what he expected me to say. The bird looked nondescript. Drab.

'Weighs less than a box of matches,' said my uncle. 'Flew over ten thousand kilometres from Siberia to get here. It'll fly further than from here to the moon in its lifetime.'

I wondered how long I'd have to stay here.

My uncle lives on the city outskirts in a two bedroom weatherboard that backs onto a mountain range. At the bottom of the hill over the railway tracks is a creek, and stretched out beyond that are cane fields. Uncle John tells me that during the last cyclone, they all went under water.

I sleep on a mattress in an enclosed veranda. There's no cupboard – I live out of my suitcase. At night I lie naked under an overhead fan that goes full tilt, testing the screws that anchor it to the ceiling. I can see the moon through the window – each night it gets a little smaller as it wanes. Outside, a large mango tree drops its fruit on the ground. Bush turkeys and rats rip them to pieces. I hear scratching and gnawing at night and see torn pulp in the grass the next day. The iron roof creaks and clunks as the day heats up, and most afternoons there's a thunderstorm which steams off the hot roads. It never gets cold.

The second bedroom is used as a study. Uncle John's desk sits under the window, surrounded by books. Makeshift shelves of planks on bricks carry volumes on birds, insects, bats, butterflies, reptiles, mammals – anything zoological. Stacks of journals sit on the wooden floor and a bar fridge full of beer hums under the desk. Uncle John leaves for work before I get up. It's school holidays so I do my own thing.

After a couple of weeks I call home but no-one picks up. I figure my old man and Leah must've gone on holiday. Somewhere remote. Once, Dad took me camping for my birthday. My teacher said I'd be able to see Jupiter and Venus if the night sky was clear but I couldn't find them, and Dad wasn't interested. He wanted to take me duck shooting instead but I didn't want to. 'What's wrong with you?' he said. We ate cheese sandwiches that Leah had made. It was nice to sit with him around the fire.

'Hey Fuckface! Check this out.' Hank beckons me over. On a small hill overlooking the creek sits a caravan with flat tires. Hank lays his bike down and creeps forward. He picks up a rock.

Hank lives a few streets over. I met him last week at the shops and he's been showing me around. He's a bit older than me.

Yesterday, we had a mango fight with some kids in Cassowary Street. Then we jumped the back fence of a big house up the hill. No-one was home so we swam in the pool. There was a little black and white terrier in the yard – a 'Ratdog,' my Dad would've called it. Hank chucked him into the pool and kept throwing him back in the middle whenever he paddled to the edge. This was pretty funny for a while, but it got to the stage where I didn't know if Hank was going to stop, so I pulled a couple of my uncle's beer cans out of my bag to distract him. When the dog finally dragged himself out, he went over to Hank for a pat. We drank a can each, and offered some to the dog, but it wasn't interested. I pretended to enjoy dangling my feet in the water but I was scared the owners would turn up.

'You don't talk much, do ya?' said Hank.

I couldn't think what to say back to him.

'How long you here?' he asked.

'Dunno,' I said. 'Maybe another week. School starts soon.'

'Ever seen snow?'

'Yeah,' I said, 'I'm from Tassie.'

'Tomorrow I wanna show you something,' he said.

Then he pissed into the pool. I pulled my feet out.

Last night Uncle John cooked a curry. He got me to cut up some beef into chunks. Then he fried them in a pan with onions and spices and simmered it in vegetable stock and tomatoes. He taught me how to wash the rice before steaming it.

'Takes the starch out,' he said.

Dropping papadums into hot oil and watching them slowly curl was my favourite bit. My uncle showed me how to press down gently with a spatula to keep them flat. I fried up a stack.

'Give me a hand after dinner eh?' he asked from across the kitchen.

'Okay,' I replied.

'I wanna move all my books into the veranda,' he said.

I stopped fishing out cutlery. Uncle John had his back to me, spooning curry into bowls.

'Where will I sleep?' I asked.

'In the study,' said my uncle. 'We'll make it your bedroom.'

Over dinner, Uncle John alternated his attention between curry and beer while I crunched my way through some papadums. There were things I wanted to ask him, but I wasn't sure how and I was scared of the answers.

'Where's Dad?' I said.

My uncle sat back in his chair and wiped his hands up and down on his shorts. Then he lifted his head and looked right at me. His scar stood out against his tanned face but he didn't look mean.

'Back in the mines,' he said.

The words hung in the air for a while and I tried to unpick them.

'But he's stopped doing that,' I said. 'He's back home now. For good.'

My uncle didn't say anything.

'What about Leah?' I asked. 'Where's she?'

'I don't know mate.'

Late afternoon the next day I cycled down to Hanks. His two brothers were doing backflips off the veranda and his Mum was mowing the backyard. I found Hank in the garage searching through a pile of junk. He pulled out an old cricket bat and tied it onto his bike rack.

'Do you like music?' he asked.

'Sure.'

'What do you listen to?'

Nothing came to mind. We didn't play much music at home.

'I don't know,' I said. 'Whatever sounds good.'

Although the sun was dipping, the heat was still strong. I stepped over clumps of prickles as we wheeled our bikes across the lawn. Hank walked right over them. After three weeks, my feet had toughened up, but nothing compared to Hank. His feet were pure callus. He reckoned he could put a cigarette out on them.

We cycled down the hill and stopped at the edge of Kamerunga Road. Trucks and four-wheel-drives barrelled past on the cracked bitumen. The air smelled of molasses from the sugar mill, and mountains loomed in the distance. When there was a break in the traffic, we crossed, bumping our way over the train tracks and freewheeling across the causeway. We pedalled up a narrow track that ran between the creek and paddocks of sugar cane.

'Ever had a fuck?' Hank asked out of the blue.

I replied honestly. After all I was only thirteen.

'Me neither,' said Hank. We kept pedalling.

'Ever seen anyone doing it?' he added.

'Nup.' I didn't want to talk about stuff like that.

Hank threw a rock at the caravan perched on the hill. It pinged off the front door. Nothing moved.

'Captain Jack lives there', said Hank. 'Old navy bloke with a wooden leg.'

'A wooden leg?'

'Yeah, like a pirate. No bullshit. I reckon he's been in jail. He used to have a cockatoo. Taught it how to say "not guilty." My brother reckons he's a kiddy fiddler.'

I couldn't think of what to say.

Hank laughed. 'Don't worry,' he said. 'No-one's home. His car's not here.'

'How does he drive with one leg?'

'Must use an automatic, eh?' said Hank. 'Pussy.'

We rode down a dirt track between fields of cane the height of two men. The air was tacky and my t-shirt stuck to my back. I wondered why we were pedalling away from the creek and not towards it – why everything went opposite to how I wanted.

Hank hopped off his bike and untied the cricket bat. He hit it against a cane stalk until it split, then levered out a piece of fibre from inside. I followed Hank's lead and chewed it for a bit – sucked out the juice and spat out the woody pulp. Tasted a bit like vanilla. Then Hank pulled out a cigarette lighter and crouched down. He laid the tiny flame against some leaf litter at the base of the sugar cane. Black smoke drifted in thin fingers.

'This is what I wanted to show you,' he said.

We kept cycling but Hank stopped regularly to light more fires. Over my shoulder I could see plumes of black smoke drifting over the cane and heard the light crackle of fire catching.

When we reached the end of the track, Hank hooked right and kept pedalling. I struggled to keep up. Once we got at the opposite side of the paddock from where the first fire was lit, he hopped off his bike. We shared a drink of water and waited.

Hank told me that his great grandfather was kidnapped from the Solomon Islands to work in the cane fields and how his grandad and old man worked their whole lives there too. He told me that back in the day they'd have a big burn-off before the harvest – how snakes and rats, scorpions, wasps and bandicoots all lived in the cane, and that during the burn-off, the hawks and eagles circled, looking for an easy feed when the animals tried to escape.

By now the sun had dropped and a breeze had kicked up. Black smoke swept over the field, and flakes of ash and cinders swirled high in the twilight. The fire howled as it intensified and flames shot ten metres out of the cane tops and thickened into a block of fire.

Hank stood ready with the cricket bat in his hand, his forehead shone, and overhead, a couple of hawks hovered. A rat shot past. Then another. Up the track I saw a snake slide into the next paddock. Then a bandicoot hopped out of the cane and stopped in front of us. The smell of burning fur and burnt sugar hit my nostrils. Hank stepped forward and clubbed the animal over the head. I turned away and started coughing from the smoke and heard the bandicoot get hit again.

'Why did you do that?' I yelled, over the roar of the fire.

'Put it out of its misery!' he yelled back at me.

Another bandicoot scuttled out and Hank cracked it across the skull. Then he picked it up by the tail and lobbed it into the blaze – turned to me with a big smile on his face.

The smoke increased as the wind gusted and I shielded my face from the heat. Another bandicoot hobbled out of the fire. One side of it was burnt raw and there was something wrong with its back leg. The animal paused on the track between the two paddocks – one green, one ablaze. Hank handed me the bat. I looked at the mountains and wished I was somewhere else. Hank grabbed the bandicoot by the tail but it didn't struggle so he let go and stepped backwards. I didn't want to hit him more than once so I lifted the bat high.

My old man wouldn't think I had it in me. I tried to think of when father's face didn't have a disappointed expression. I remembered a few years back when some miners were trapped underground in Chile. I couldn't sleep at night, and he'd scoffed.

'Don't worry about me,' he said. 'I just drive the trucks.'

But I wasn't worried about him – I knew he drove trucks. I wasn't stupid. I worried for the men in the dark. The men underground – whether they'd be buried alive.

I swung the bat down hard. Far away, Hank was yelling but I kept hitting the little animal. Then an ember scorched the top of my hand and I stopped. Plumes of sparks poured into the sky and the bandicoot lay in a lumpy mess at my feet. My eyes started to water. They streamed. The fire had leapt to the green paddock and began to flare-up. Hank was jumping up and down, yelling and waving at the end of the track – a shimmering figure through heat and smoke. I watched hairs on my arms pucker and shrivel and heard booming thunder and sirens in the distance.

We zig-zagged through spot fires, raining ash and falling embers, back towards the creek. Bikes abandoned, our feet flopped in warm black ash.

'Snow! yelled Hank. 'Black snow!'

Rain fell on my face. Pouring rain.

When Uncle John woke me later that night it was pitch black and the rain had stopped. The world was quiet. I was in my new bedroom. I don't know what the time was.

'Get dressed and get in the car,' said my uncle. He handed me the jacket and jeans I'd worn when I first arrived.

We drove for about an hour. Out of town and into the mountains. The moon had vanished and it was difficult to make out if the sky was overcast, or totally clear. As the Landrover swept around each hairpin, the headlights briefly illuminated thick forest. Sometimes I glimpsed the coast out my window – far, far below. A dim gleam on dark water. The city lights twinkled lightly on the fringe before fading into nothing, and the top of my hand throbbed where it had been burned. A bandage of gauze and surgical tape covered the injury. Uncle John must have dressed the wound last night, but I don't remember this happening. I tried to remember my father's face, but was having difficulty. Uncle John kept driving onwards and upwards, corner after corner. I nodded off.

When I was shaken awake, the car had stopped, and the engine was off. I felt cold. First time I'd been cold since Tasmania. Reaching out, I touched the chill of the windscreen. I couldn't see my uncle in the darkness, but I heard him beside me.

'Here,' he said, guiding my fingers around a container. 'Watch yourself. It's a thermos.'

I had a sip. Hot chocolate. I thanked him.

Uncle John got out and closed his door. He crunched around the bonnet, to my side. He helped me get out.

'Hold my hand,' he said. I gave him my good one.

My feet pressed into mud and twigs as he led me up a track. Sometimes he paused to push aside a branch or help me over a log. The forest thrummed with the drone of insects and frogs, the dripping of water, the flapping of wings. Sporadic crashes sounded in the thickets – animals or fallen branches. The earth groaned with life. The blackness was crushing. I couldn't sense depth or distance and allowed myself to be pulled along.

Then my uncle slowed and let go of my hand. I stepped forward and stood by his side. In the distance, floating in the night, was something from dreams. A horizontal plane of pulsing light. Luminescence. Blues and greens, yellows and whites – like jewels. We stepped closer. My uncle's face looked like a child's – like how I felt. In wonder. He put his arm around me and drew me in close. He gripped me. We stood in front of the bank cutting, thick with glow worms. A glittering universe stretched out before us.

Dizz Tate

Dizz Tate won the Bristol Short Story Prize in 2018. Her debut novel, *Brutes,* was published in 2023 by Faber in the UK and Catapult in the US.

COWBOY BOOT

The jungle gym was a gift from Richard Turnball to his little stepdaughter, two weeks before his plane went down on a private flight from Cleveland to Colorado. Turnball was a flight attendant, which Mary, who lived opposite, had always politely thought was a profession for ladies, no offence intended.

The bodies could not be identified, mangled with metal and burns, but they retrieved a few molars, and found a white, gold-trimmed cowboy boot a few miles away on a mountain, miraculously whole, and undeniably Turnball's, his name having even been printed on the bottom by his doting wife, Jillian, some months before. The cowboy boot was delivered to Jillian by First-Class mail, and became somewhat of a sensation in the state press, the Miracle Boot From the Mountain. Jillian was not in any of the photographs, but her little girl was, holding the boot and looking morose. Mary thought this doubly distasteful, as after all, she was not even his true child. Jillian wailed noisily for weeks after she received the boot, even though his death had been pretty much certain for months already. Sometimes Mary thought she understood this behaviour, and sometimes she didn't understand it at all.

The jungle gym from Turnball was right next to Mary's house, in the only empty lot in the neighbourhood. The forces that ran the community had wanted to uproot it back across to the Turnball's driveway ('Why would he dump it on someone else's property?' they asked each other, over and over, 'He's got a perfectly good yard!') but after his death, the jungle gym remained, and the lot stayed empty, out of some form of respect, though none of the kids even used it, there being the community centre just three streets away with a playground three times the size.

It was some weeks after the boot delivery when Mary watched Jillian and her little girl cross the street toward her porch and the lot. She sat up a little straighter. Jillian held a shovel and her little girl held the famous boot. The girl darted up the jungle gym and sat on the top of the slide, holding the boot like a baby, while Jillian began to dig a hole at the bottom. Jillian was a small, birdy woman, and the digging took her a long time. She could barely shift the dirt, hard-packed as it was from the cold.

Mary sat in the chair in her porch and watched her as she dug more and more wildly, sweat forming a thick sheen on her forehead. She thought of the times she had seen Turnball careening down the street in the family Ford. She had seen him passed out in every front yard in the street – everyone knew he'd turned thick from liquor. A few times he had been with other people, shadows in the passenger seat. They would park in front of the jungle gym and seem to just talk. Mary was not fooled. She had seen enough to know that talking could be the most dangerous kind of work.

She had been working out how to tell Jillian about her husband's indiscretions when he died in the plane crash. She felt both relieved and a little bitter at her missed opportunity. Mary was known for passing on damaging information at the most brittle of times. She saw a lot – sitting all day in her screened-in porch, the Turnball's opposite, Georgia May and her little pretty family next to them. The other house she could see most clearly was the rental house – full of strangers for weeks in the summer, and thus a cauldron of gossip. Mary found the vacationers fascinating. They were so odd. One young couple liked to climb on the roof and sunbathe naked. Another family wore turbans. Another had a little boy and girl who played at murdering each other in the driveway, acting out a hundred different deaths, while their father stood in the doorway, filming them on his phone.

While Jillian dug the hole, the little girl sucked her thumb on the top of the slide. She'd suck for a second, then spit over her shoulder. Suck and spit. Disgusting, thought Mary, but the mother just kept pushing her shovel into the dirt and did not chastise the girl.

Some of the other mothers came and stood around. Mrs. Hutchinson, who was Mary's age, and she thought, too old to be involved in these types of tragedies, brought a bottle of whisky, which she passed around in paper cups. The mothers stood around Jillian who continued to dig as though they were not there. No one offered to help her, but occasionally one or the other would dart a quick hand to slap Jillian's shoulder. Mary thought they looked like crows, ravenous to peck at a non-existent seed.

Mrs. Hutchinson came up to Mary's screen door after a while and tipped the whisky bottle to her. 'Can't tempt you, Mary?' she said. Mary shook her head, pulled her blanket to her neck, but Mrs. Hutchinson opened the screen door anyway, sat cross-legged like a child on the floor of her porch.

'You're a saint, lady Mary,' she said, slurring. Mary looked past her, watched as Georgia May, the prettiest woman on the street, with a teenagers face at forty, swung an arm round Jillian.

'Looks deep enough,' said Georgia May.

Jillian's face scrunched itself up. She sat on the ground, looked at the little girl who took her thumb from her mouth, slid down the slide, expertly braking with her feet to stop herself at the bottom before hitting the hole. She placed the boot in the earth, stuck her thumb back in her mouth, spat.

'Aren't you a little old for thumb-sucking?' called Mrs. Hutchinson to the girl. Mary blushed. The girl looked at them for a second, then down again at the hole. She put her hands in her coat pockets.

'Oh, shut up, would you?' said Mary to Mrs. Hutchinson. The jungle gym shined in the winter sunlight. She strained to hear Jillian.

'Perhaps we should have burnt it,' she said. 'But burying seemed more – oh, I don't know –.'

'Significant,' said Georgia May. She took the shovel gently from Jillian's hands, gave her a plastic cup to hold.

Georgia May's daughter, a cheeky kid in a boy's tuxedo jacket, hair curling in under her chin, wandered up to the hole. Mary watched as she whispered something to Jillian's little girl, who looked up at her, expressionless, then offered a dazzling smile.

Oh, I wish I knew what she said, thought Mary.

'The little ones are so much different than us, aren't they, Mary?' said Mrs. Hutchinson. 'They're surely not gonna listen to you when you tell them about their cheating husbands. They'll probably be the cheaters themselves.'

'Oh, be quiet, you drunk old bat,' said Mary, and Mrs. Hutchinson laughed.

'Look up!' cried Georgia May's little girl, suddenly. Georgia May, Jillian, Mrs. Hutchinson, Mary, and the few other women all looked up. A sheer arc of starlings contracted and expanded across the waxy blue sky.

'There's Richard,' said Jillian. 'There's Richard waving to me.'

Mrs. Hutchinson tutted, and said, low under her breath so only Mary could hear, 'That old fag is a boot in the ground and nothing else now.'

Mary chuckled. Pushing herself from her chair, she walked to the other side of the screen porch and sat in the chair that used to belong to her husband. She still got a faint sense of unease sitting in it – once, years before he died, she had sunk herself down into it and refused to move, even while he worked himself up into a fit, ('That's my chair! My chair!'), his hands in fists he was never going to throw.

'Sit in a chair, for goodness sake, woman,' she said now to Mrs. Hutchinson, who struggled upright and sat in the vacated chair, her feet curled girlishly beneath her.

Mary looked over the length of the street, the icy black tarmac and the beige houses lined up, neat and well-behaved looking as show dogs. She looked for the girls, but they had gone, disappeared into one house or another, and she thought for a long time while Mrs. Hutchinson slurred her way to sleep beside her, just what it was that the one had whispered to the other, to make her smile that way.

Brent van Staalduinen

Brent van Staalduinen is the award-winning author of the novels *Unthinkable, Nothing But Life, Boy,* and *Saints, Unexpected,* as well as the short story collection *Cut Road.* He is the winner of the Kerry Schooley Book Award, the 2015 Bristol Short Story Prize, the Fiddlehead Best Story Award, the Lush Triumphant Literary Award, and numerous other prizes, and his stories can be found in journals on both sides of the Atlantic. A former high school English teacher, library staff member, radio announcer, army medic, and tree planter, Brent now finds himself helping university writing students discover their voices and lives in Hamilton, Ontario, Canada, with his wife and two daughters. He is also the creator and co-host of Rejected Central, a podcast which explores the history, pain, and humour of rejection. www.brentvans.com, www.rejectedcentral.com, @brentvans.

A WEEK ON
THE WATER

A few weeks ago, I asked to work days but the manager just smirked. I told him it was a bitch to get buses up the escarpment late at night and that sleeping through the day made it hard to see my son. He balled up my kelly green apron and flung it against my chest. I almost dropped it, its ties cascading from my hands halfway to the floor like entrails. "Guess you shouldn't have messed up so bad, then," he said.

All you can do is ask, I think, waiting for the tip of my fishing rod to dance.

I don't argue any more. It's a hard habit to break but that former edge, the strongest and most successful part of myself, won't help me. Better for it to sit in my stomach like a river stone – one of the native guys inside said that if you swallow enough of them the appetite goes away. He didn't seem like he was particularly plugged in to the spirit side of things and was probably making things up as he went – like all of us – but I guess the idea works just fine, apart from wondering where the stones will end up.

"Greenie still giving you grief?"

Gram's cigarette dances on his lower lip with every syllable. I met him almost a week ago. He's out fishing every day too.

"Always," I say.

"That whole place is green," he said on Tuesday. I had just told him about the supermarket where I worked nights and he went straight to the colour scheme. I didn't say much, but I told him about the manager who makes me sign my paycheque over to him every two weeks then pays me in cash, significantly reduced. "After taxes," he always says with a sneer. Yesterday, Gram decided to call him Greenie.

He spits.

"God, I hate that part of the city. Did I tell you I used to have a house up there, right across the street from all those big box stores?"

"No," I say.

He smiles. His teeth used to be perfect, I can see.

"Yeah, paid for that bad boy in cash. All those fat, bored housewives looking for a little something. Suburban junkies – best market ever."

"You don't live up there any more."

A dark look deepens his features, fleeting, and he gives a lipless smile. But he doesn't reply. You learn not to ask when they're not offering, so I take a small piece of chicken liver and thread it onto the treble hook.

We're on the harbour side of the fishway, next to the recreation path, dropping for catfish. The secret is the bait; it has to be smelly and full of proteins so the cats can find it. Gram's working some old Fancy Feast cat food in surgical tubing and he's had better luck. He said I could try some of his, but my grandfather swore by liver and I'm stubborn about these things. Still, I haven't caught a thing, a week of lob cast after lob cast and waiting while the current dilutes the juices in the meat before having to do it all over again. There's something about loyalty, though.

I don't mind the job, despite my douchebag boss. The store's open twenty-four hours a day but most of the restocking happens overnight, when there are fewer customers to get in the way. They have to pay a night manager, a cashier, and a small army of guys who need to work at night: even though they only open one checkout and dim the lights in the storeroom I can't imagine how they make any money. Not my call – in my former life I'd have cringed at the business model, unknowing that one moment of weakness and seven long years would erase the need to worry about anything greater than working a night shift, getting to bed afterwards, and channel fishing as daily therapy.

Gram's rig dips and drifts. He picks it up from the little rack he's spiked into the ground and holds it away from himself, eyes closed, feeling the bite. A quick upward pull to set the hook and the fish, feeling the tug, tries to run towards the harbour. It's all over in less than a minute. Such a narrow channel and there's nowhere to go, and the fish can't fathom the disparity in physics between the rod and reel and its own finite strength. It's a good one, three or four pounds, and Gram lifts it out of the water with a thumb in its gaping mouth. A thin line of bright red blood runs down its grey belly and drips steadily onto the gravel shoreline. The fish gives a weak twitch of its tail, flinging blood all over.

"Ah, shit, I hate it when they bleed," he says, holding the cat away from his body and wiping the hem of his rain jacket.

"He'll bleed out, I think."

"Yeah, we hooked the gills."

Using the treble hook is a conscious choice. Cats almost always swallow the small trebles whole and the points work hell on their insides. Some guys bend and break off the barbs at each razor point but we don't, preferring a good hook set to the more sporting approach of catch-and-release. Gram likes the taste of catfish but admits that he's too lazy to take them home and clean them. I'd do it, but the halfway house frowns on the mess and smell of gutting and frying the catch. If they live, we toss them back into the channel; if they don't, we leave them out for the birds and animals to take care of. But it's been a cold few days, so maybe the animals can't smell the ones Gram gill-hooked and left to die pale, bloodless deaths.

We still have the conversation we've had all week, though.

"You gonna do something with this one?"

"Can't," he says.

"Me neither."

On Wednesday, I learned that Gram changed his name after he dropped out from college to deal full-time ("I used to be a Graham," he laughed. "Get it?"). It was a really slow fishing day, kind of windy and choppy on the harbour side, so we set up on the marsh side next to the fishway. They set up a barrier across the Desjardins Canal to act like a sieve, keeping the mature carp, big suckers who feed on the bottom, from swimming in and upsetting the plant life. Hard to believe one species can ruin so much water. I don't think either of us got even a nibble from the native marsh fish. Gram did most of the talking that day. Most days, actually – not arguing so much any more leaves a lot less for me to say.

Gram pulls out a joint the size of my pinkie and asks if I want to spark up. I shake my head, conscious of the weekend cyclists and rollerbladers hissing past.

"Relax, man, we're too far down the trail."

He giggles – a grating sound in the cool air – and tries to light it. It's calm today, the birds making perfect mirror images of themselves on the channel, but damp too, so the J won't stay lit. After a few tries he swears, the scorched tip bouncing like the head of an impatient, greasy maggot.

Then it's the tip of my rod bowing towards the algae-green water and I'm up trying to set the hook. But it pulls too easy. I missed the hit, figure the cat must've nabbed the liver and spat it out before I could hook him. I reel it in, the bright sinker emerging from the underwater gloom followed by the leader and treble. Bare, as though the fish's tongue was able to weave itself around and through the barbs gently enough to take the bait but not get caught.

"Took my bait," I say as I pinch and skewer another bit of bloody liver.

Gram doesn't say anything. Unusual. Just before I lob out my rig, I look over at him. He's zoned right out, staring at the far bank, through the ground, maybe, or into the past he talks about so much I wonder if he's lying. Just to have a story. I knew guys like that inside, so wrecked they'd talk and talk even after getting beaten up for saying the wrong thing. There was this one guy who walked up to the new ones at intake and told each of them a different story about how he ended up there. One day I watched him get his head caved in by a skinhead who probably wasn't even listening but needed to hurt someone anyhow.

I wave my hand in front of his face. Nothing.

"Don't bother when he gets like that – too much of his own product for too long," a voice says from behind.

A pair of bike cops, top-heavy in body armour and utility belts and bright yellow jackets, have ridden up without a sound and stopped at the edge of the paved path behind us. Spindly legs, ridiculous black socks and safety shoes, wraparound sunglasses. I almost laugh but the J is still hanging from Gram's mouth, and the one who spoke, the bigger one, looks like the type to get worked up over a single joint.

"Isn't that right, Gram?"

Gram blinks a few times and turns towards the cops. He gives a dopey smile, looks past the big one, and tilts his head in a hopeful greeting towards the other guy.

"Hey, Wharton."

"Gram."

Wharton, the smaller one who's as pale as our dead fish on the shoreline, says this without taking his eyes from the water on the other side of the fishway. He leans across the handlebars of his police-issue mountain bike and simply studies Cootes Paradise like he's thinking about taking his next holiday there. Gram slips the J into his pocket, but neither of the cops says anything about that. He fidgets. A tight soundtrack of spare change and hidden keys. The big guy nods at me and asks me my name.

The new me grits his teeth and tells him.

"Holy fuck! Almost a week of fishing and I never even knew his name!"

Gram's too excited, hoping this new interesting tidbit will distract everyone, maybe. The big cop dismounts, clicks down the kickstand and steps unevenly across the stones to the edge of the water. Turns towards me, takes off his glasses, and scratches a patch of missed stubble with a fingernail. The arms of his Oakleys swing and knock against his chin with each scratch.

"Anything biting?"

"Not today, no."

Now that he's closer he looks even bigger. His expensive sunglasses have stencilled tan lines on his cheekbones. I don't have to ask to know there are equally sharp lines on his thick biceps and thighs and calves; a creature of routine, every item of uniform put on the same way every time. He doesn't look like the type of guy to be a bike cop – he'd look more at home squeezed behind the steering wheel of one of those smaller new cruisers and harassing kids on skateboards.

"We heard you were out," he says. "Shame they couldn't put you somewhere else."

Wharton is ignoring the waves of cliché his partner is putting out. He's closed his eyes and turned his face towards the muddy sun trying to peek through the clouds. Gram fidgets next to me, a sparrow trying not to get noticed as it hops between tables looking for crumbs. I don't say anything, just dangle the liver-baited rig over the water and lob it out. It sinks without a ripple. I sit back down onto my blue Igloo cooler.

"Are we going to have any trouble with you?"

I shake my head, taking exactly one second for each side to keep the redness from blinding me.

"No, sir."

"No, sir," Gram parrots.

As the big one nods and starts back to his bike, Wharton begins to speak, never opening his eyes or turning his face away from the warmth he's found, and suddenly I know which of these two I'm really going to have to worry about.

"See, that's the thing about the big ones – trafficking, rape, homicide – what actually happens looks so different after the courts get done with it."

Two of those were meant for me. Gram took the other in with a little whimper, his brag and bluster dissolved like sugar in hot water.

"And it concerns me to find you here, close enough to the home you've been ordered to stay away from that it's obvious you're not ready to move on, but far enough away that you could honestly say it's about the fishing."

Gram's shoulders relax and he studies the place where his line disappears into the water. I can almost hear him clueing in that the cops aren't really concerned about him at all.

"Your record says you're smart. Clever too, maybe. But, then, I was never a fan of clever," Wharton finishes.

I don't argue any more, I want to say.

Wharton opens his eyes and takes another long look at the calm water on the other side of the fishway, waiting for his partner to mount his bike. Then the cops pedal slowly away, nodding and smiling at the pedestrians and other cyclists on the harbour side of the path, ringing their handlebar bells for the kids. Gram fishes quietly beside me having decided, I know, to wait until later to Google his new fishing friend. I probably won't see him tomorrow, Sunday, my last day of work and fishing before my Monday off. I'll go back to hooking channel cats on my own and watching the path, hoping someone in that home will decide that it's a nice enough day for a walk, maybe, down by the marsh.

Acknowledgements

THANK YOU: Sami Al-Adawy, Irene Baldoni, Georgia Bate, Diane Becker, Peter Begen, John Bennett, Joe Berger, Sam Bevington, Bidisha, Martin Booth, Jo Borek, Harry Boucher, Nick Bright, Maia Bristol, Anna Britten, Andi Bullard, Joe Burt, Dr Edson Burton, Joanna Campbell, Prof John Carey, Imogen Cheetham, Annette Chown, Naomi Clarke, Imogen Clifton, Nicky Coates, Sophie Collard, Liz Conquest, Jennifer Cope, Lucy Cowie, Jo Darque, Sara Davies, Tom Dodge, Tom Drake-Lee, Jessie Eames, Vic Ecclestone, Gary Embury, Stuart Evers, Susan Eyles, Abi Fellows, Patricia Ferguson, Roshi Fernando, Dan Franklin, Prof Helen Fulton, Mark Furneval, Janice Galloway, Vanessa Gebbie, Beccy Golding, Dr Paul Gough, Andy Gove, Niven Govinden, Martyna Gradziel, Ellen Grant, Ali Griffiths, Jane Guy, Zoe Hall, Fran Ham, Andy Hamilton, Katherine Hanks, Mel Harris, Helen Hart, Robin Haward, Angela Haward, David Hebblethwaite, Tania Hershman, Lu Hersey, Clare Hey, Sarah Hilary, Chris Hill, Polly Ho-Yen, Sandra Hopkins, Jeanette Jarvie, Kate Johnson, Alice Jones, Richard Jones, Dr Billy Kahora, Nik Kalinowski, Gruff Kennedy, Simon Key, Sylvie Kruiniger, Nick Law, Rowan Lawton, Helen Legg, Amy Lehain, Marc Leverton, Jonathan Lewis, Miranda Lewis, Kirsty Logan, Lynn Love, Sharmaine Lovegrove, Prof Mary Luckhurst, Anneliese Mackintosh, Alison Macleod, Dr Sam Matthews, Mike Manson, Heather Marks, Bertel Martin, Amy Mason, Catherine Mason, Eva Mason, Kathy

McDermot, Robin McDowell, Patricia McNair, Louis Melia, Rosa Melia, Tash Melia, Peter Morgan, Sam Morrison, Bea Moyes, Emily Nash, Courttia Newland, Emma Newman, Dave Oakley, Roisin Oakley, Sanjida O'Connell, Irenosen Okojie, Helen Oyeyemi, Scott Pack, Ra Page, Cassandra Parkin, Eleanor Pender, Juliet Pickering, Dawn Pomroy, Gareth L Powell, Lisa Price, Aitana Raguán-Hernández, Thomas Rasche, Prof Marie Mulvey-Roberts, Tom Robinson, Dan Ross, Sarah Salway, Angela Sansom, John Sansom, Sarah Salway, Gaby Selby, Claire Shorrock, Tim Shute, Nikesh Shukla, Pam Smallwood, Mahsuda Smaith, Joe Spurgeon, Harry Sussams, Joshua Tallent, Rosanna Tasker, Jess Taylor, Keith Taylor, Dr Mimi Thebo, Liz Tressider, Sam Usher, Valentina Vinci, Berni Vinton, Megan Vowles, Emily Wade, Chris Wakling, Isabelle Wallace, Jonathan Ward, Franki Webb, Sol Wilkinson, D W Wilson, Lucy Wood, Chris Woollatt, Anna Wredenfors.

And biggest thanks to all the writers who have had the courage to enter the Bristol Short Story Prize competitions and share their stories with us. Thank you for giving us such wonderful reading experiences and ensuring the short story continues to flourish.